Hello and welcome!

*Vor dir liegt der **Wordmaster**. Er hilft dir beim Wörterlernen.*

*Sobald du neue Wörter in der Schule besprochen hast, mach die **New words and phrases** in diesem Heft.*

*Die **fett gedruckten** deutschen Wörter sind Lernwörter. Sie fehlen im englischen Satz, damit du sie eintragen kannst.*

*Im Anschluss an die **New words and phrases** gibt es kurze Aufgaben, Rätsel und Wortspiele, mit denen du den neuen Wortschatz übst und festigst.*

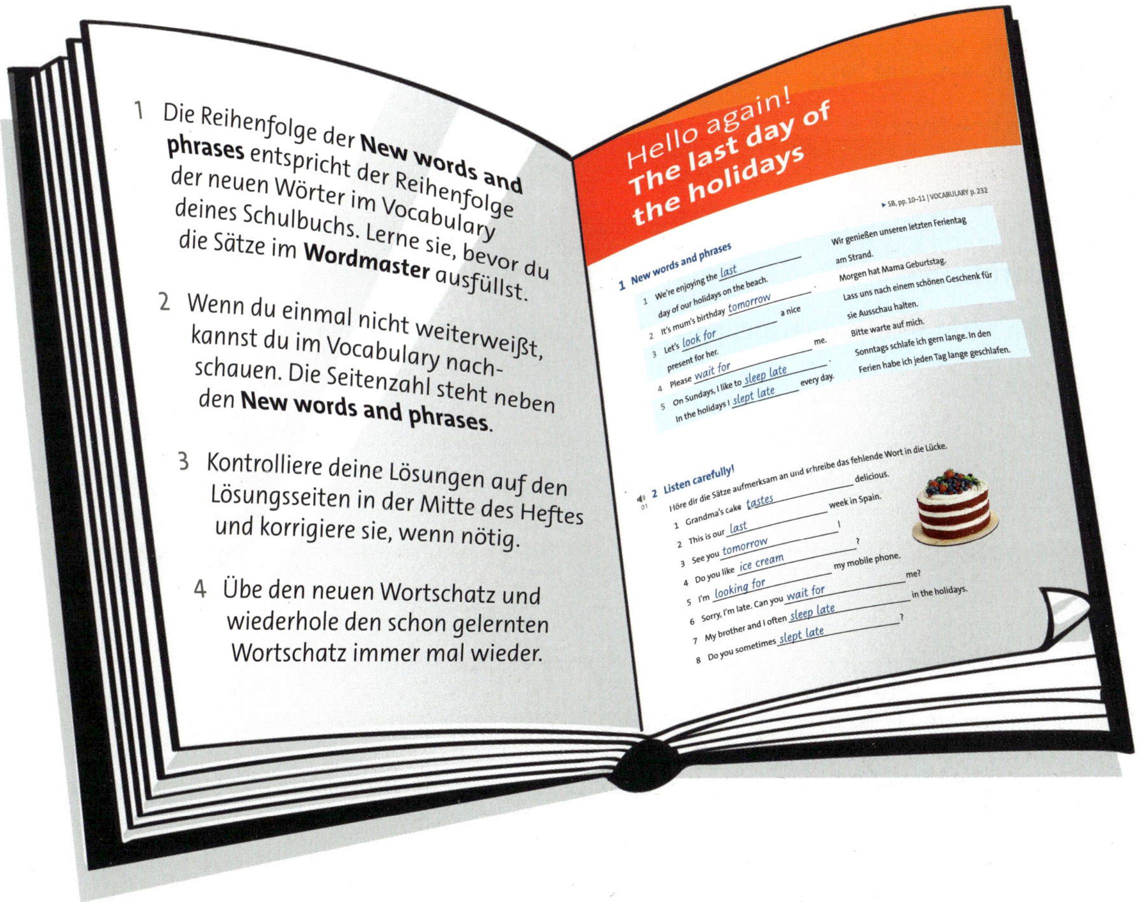

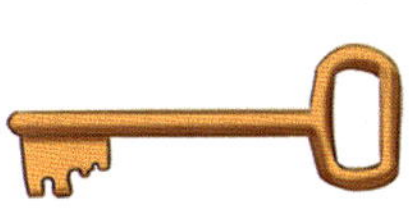

Alle Lösungen findest du auf den Lösungsseiten in der Mitte des Heftes. Die Hörtexte 🔊 zu den Listen carefully!-Aufgaben kannst du in deiner Cornelsen Lernen App aufrufen. Dort findest du auch noch einmal die Lösungen.

Hello again!
The last day of the holidays

1 New words and phrases

▸ SB, pp. 10–11 | VOCABULARY p. 232

1	We're enjoying the ____________ day of our holidays on the beach.	Wir genießen unseren **letzten** Urlaubstag am Strand.
2	It's mum's birthday ____________.	**Morgen** hat Mama Geburtstag.
3	Let's ____________ a nice present for her.	Lass uns **nach** einem schönen Geschenk für sie **Ausschau halten**.
4	Please ____________ me.	Bitte **warte auf** mich.
5	On Sundays, I like to ____________. In the holidays I ____________ every day.	Sonntags **schlafe** ich gern **lange**. In den Ferien **habe** ich jeden Tag **lange geschlafen**.

2 Listen carefully!

01

Höre dir die Sätze aufmerksam an und schreibe das fehlende Wort in die Lücke.

1 Grandma's cake ____________ delicious.

2 This is our ____________ week in Spain.

3 See you ____________!

4 Do you like ____________?

5 I'm ____________ my mobile phone.

6 Sorry, I'm late. Can you ____________ me?

7 My brother and I often ____________ in the holidays.

8 Do you sometimes ____________?

▸ Check

Unit 1
Travel and holidays

1 New words and phrases

► SB, pp. 12–13 | VOCABULARY pp. 232–233

1	Last week ____________ in England with my class.	Letzte Woche **war ich** mit meiner Klasse in England.
2	It was my first school ____________.	Es war mein erster Schul**ausflug**.
3	____________ in Brighton and in London.	**Wir waren** in Brighton und in London.
4	____________ away in the holidays.	**Ich war nicht** weg in den Ferien.
5	____________ at home last week.	**Wir waren** letzte Woche **nicht** zu Hause.
6	London is Britain's ____________.	London ist Großbritanniens **Haupstadt**.
7	Ben Nevis is a high ____________ in Scotland.	Ben Nevis ist ein hoher **Berg** in Schottland.
8	You can see Ben Nevis from the ____________ near Fort William.	Man kann Ben Nevis vom **Campingplatz** bei Fort William aus sehen.
9	My family and I were in a holiday ____________ in Brighton.	Meine Familie und ich waren in einer Ferien**wohnung** in Brighton.
10	The sea was ____________ cold.	Das Meer war **ein bisschen** kalt.

2 New words and phrases

► SB, p. 14 | VOCABULARY p. 233

1	Mia sometimes ____________ with a friend at the weekend.	Am Wochenende **übernachtet** Mia manchmal bei einer Freundin.
2	There are lots of beaches at the British coast where you can ____________.	Es gibt viele Strände an der britischen Küste, an denen man **sonnenbaden** kann.
3	Tom's ____________ is British, his ____________ is German.	Toms **Mutter** ist Britin, sein **Vater** ist Deutscher.
4	I have a problem with my right ____________.	Ich habe ein Problem mit meinem rechten **Fuß**.
5	Don't put your dirty ____________ on the sofa!	Leg deine schmutzigen **Füße** nicht aufs Sofa!

3 New words and phrases

▸ SB, p. 15 | VOCABULARY p. 233

1	Mia's ____________ live in the country.	Mias **Großeltern** wohnen auf dem Land.
2	We often take the ____________ from Dunkerque in France to Dover in Britain.	Wir nehmen oft die **Fähre** von Dünkirchen in Frankreich nach Dover in Großbritannien.
3	You can also go to Britain by ____________.	Man kann auch mit dem **Flugzeug** nach Großbritannien reisen.
4	There is a restaurant on the top of the ____________.	Es gibt ein Restaurant oben auf dem **Hügel**.
5	The Thames is a big ____________.	Die Themse ist ein großer **Fluss**.
6	We live ____________.	Wir wohnen **am Fluss**.

4 New words and phrases

▸ SB, p. 16 | VOCABULARY p. 234

1	What ____________ books do you read?	Welche **Art von** Büchern liest du?
2	You can do ____________ sports at our school.	Man kann **alle möglichen** Sportarten an unserer Schule machen.
3	The film is too ____________ for kids.	Der Film ist zu **gruselig** für Kinder.
4	It started to rain ____________ we were in the park.	Es fing an zu regnen, **als** wir im Park waren.
5	Do you like ____________ stories?	Magst du **Geister**geschichten?
6	I don't go out when it's ____________.	Ich gehe nicht raus, wenn es **dunkel** ist.
7	Are you scared of ____________?	Hast du Angst vor **Vampiren**?
8	Mum makes funny ____________.	Mama macht lustige **Kostüme**.
9	Can we go on an ____________ tour?	Können wir eine Tour **unter der Erde** machen?
10	____________ there were lions in Germany.	**Vor langer Zeit** gab es in Deutschland Löwen.
11	My brother always ____________ when he doesn't get an ice cream.	Mein Bruder **schreit** immer, wenn er kein Eis bekommt.
12	Please don't ____________ my dog.	Bitte **fasse** meinen Hund nicht **an**.
13	It's too cold to go ____________.	Es ist zu kalt, um **nach draußen** zu gehen.

▸ Check

5 Word snake

Finde sechs Wörter in der Schlange und setze sie in die richtigen Lücken ein.

1 Berlin is Germany's ______________________ city.
2 I don't want to go to London by ______________________.
3 How was your class ______________________?
4 How do you like my Halloween ______________________?
5 We live in a small ______________________.
6 We stayed on a ______________________ in our holidays.

6 What's the word: *was* or *were*?

Vervollständige die Sätze mit den Wörtern aus dem Kasten.

was (2x) • wasn't • were (3x) • weren't

1 Last week my family and I ______________________ on holiday.
2 ______________________ you in the mountains?
3 No, we ______________________. We ______________________ in London.
4 ______________________ your grandma with you?
5 Yes, she ______________________, but my grandpa ______________________ with us this time.

7 Lost words

Vervollständige die Sätze mit den Wörtern aus den Luftballons.

1 I'm looking *for* my sister. Do you know where she is?
2 What sort ______________ games do you play?
3 You can go to Britain ______________ ferry.
4 Last summer Nora was in Spain ______________ her family.
5 I take the bus to school ______________ the morning.
6 Kim has football practice ______________ Friday.
7 It's very quiet here ______________ night.
8 I'm waiting ______________ my friends. They're late.
9 We went hiking ______________ the mountains this summer.
10 The Millers have a nice house ______________ the river.
11 I like sitting ______________ the beach.
12 I like playing games ______________ my friends.

► Check

8 New words and phrases

► SB, p. 17 | VOCABULARY pp. 234–235

1	This ____________ summer John worked in Italy.	Im **vergangenen** Sommer hat John in Italien gearbeitet.
2	The dog is old and ____________.	Der Hund ist alt und **blind**.
3	Let's walk home ____________ the park.	Lass uns **durch** den Park nach Hause gehen.
4	I like your vampire ____________.	Mir gefällt deine Vampir**maske**.
5	Most dogs have brown ____________.	Die meisten Hunde haben braune **Augen**.
6	It was so dark in the room that I ____________ ____________ to find the door.	Es war so dunkel im Zimmer, dass ich meine **Hände ausstreckte**, um die Tür zu finden.
7	Kim has lots of ____________ with horses.	Kim hat viel **Erfahrung** mit Pferden.
8	____________ from the station to the hotel is free.	Die **Beförderung** vom Bahnhof zum Hotel ist kostenlos.
9	What helps you to ____________?	Was hilft dir, **dich** zu **entspannen**?

9 New words and phrases

► SB, p. 18 | VOCABULARY p. 235

1	I ____________ you like the book.	Ich **hoffe**, das Buch gefällt dir.
2	Mick looked at his son with ____________.	Mick sah seinen Sohn mit **Stolz** an.
	He was ____________ of his son.	Er war **stolz** auf seinen Sohn.
3	Tom's first day at his new school was a big ____________.	Toms erster Tag an seiner neuen Schule war ein großes **Ereignis**.
4	This bike costs a ____________ euros.	Dieses Fahrrad kostet **tausend** Euro.
5	Our new ____________ time is 2 p.m.	Unsere neue **Ankunfts**zeit ist 14 Uhr.
6	What ____________ does our train go from?	Von welchem **Bahnsteig** fährt unser Zug?

10 New words and phrases

► SB, p. 19 | VOCABULARY p. 235

1	What's your next holiday ____________?	Was ist dein nächstes Urlaubs**ziel**?
2	A ____________ ticket is 2.80 €.	Eine **Einzel**fahrkarte kostet 2,80 €.
3	I need a ____________.	Ich brauche eine **Rückfahrkarte**.
4	Good bicyles aren't ____________.	Gute Fahrräder sind nicht **billig**.

► Check

11 New words and phrases

▸ SB, pp. 20–21 | VOCABULARY p. 236

1	Kim ______________ to the party.	Kim **ist nicht** auf die Party **gegangen**.
2	Liam collects ______________.	Liam sammelt **Flaggen**.
3	I ______________ hear ______________.	Ich **kann nichts** hören.
4	Where are you? I ______________ see you ______________.	Wo bist du? Ich **kann** dich **gar nicht** sehen.
5	Look, there's a ______________.	Schau mal. Da ist ein **Regenbogen**.
6	We all love loud music, ______________ our dog.	Wir alle lieben laute Musik, **sogar** unser Hund.
7	I like my brother's new ______________.	Ich mag die neue **Freundin** meines Bruders.
8	My sister doesn't have a ______________.	Meine Schwester hat keinen **Freund**.
9	We live in a quiet ______________.	Wir wohnen in einer ruhigen **Gegend**.
10	Jon's sister has one ______________, his brother has two ______________.	Jons Schwester hat ein **Kind**, sein Bruder hat zwei **Kinder**.
11	Are you going to the ______________?	Gehst du zum **Konzert**?
12	Jon's dad is a ______________.	Jons Vater ist **Musiker**.
13	Philip is a ______________ father.	Philip ist ein **wunderbarer** Vater.
14	Can you play the ______________?	Kannst du **Klavier** spielen?

02

12 Listen carefully!

Höre dir die Sätze aufmerksam an und schreibe das fehlende Wort in die Lücke.

1 We were on a nice campsite in the ______________.
2 We travelled to England by ______________.
3 My mother likes ______________.
4 Do you like ______________ stories?
5 I like stories about ______________.
6 Don't ______________ the oven. It's hot.
7 It's very ______________ outside.
8 Let's walk ______________ the park.
9 Does Mr Cox have any ______________ in teaching?
10 My cat has green ______________.

13 Letter code

Welche Buchstaben sind 1, 2, 3 und 4?

1: ____ 2: ____ 3: ____ 4: ____

1 L1st w22k I visit2d my gr14dp1r24ts.

2 Gr14dp1 k43ws 1 l3t 1b3ut tr14sp3rt.

3 H2 h2lp2d m2 with my pr2s24t1ti34 1b3ut f2rri2s.

4 I 1lw1ys th3ught th1t f2rri2s w2r2 b3ri4g, but Gr14dp1 t3ld m2 s3m2 2xciti4g thi4gs 1b3ut th2m.

14 New words and phrases

▸ SB, pp. 23–24 | VOCABULARY pp. 236–237

1	It's easy ______________________ at school.	Es ist leicht, **Freunde/Freundinnen** in der Schule **zu finden**.
2	I want to go to London to see the ______________.	Ich möchte nach London fahren und mir die **Sehenswürdigkeiten** anschauen.
3	The clock ______________ of the Palace of Westminster in London is called Elizabeth ______________. Big Ben is the name of the biggest bell in it.	Der Uhr**turm** des Westminster Palasts in London heißt Elisabeth**turm**. Big Ben ist der Name der größten Glocke darin.
4	At night our street is ______________.	Nachts ist es **still** in unserer Straße.
5	______________________ don't break.	**Plastikflaschen** zerbrechen nicht.
6	Is this beach ______________ for children?	Ist dieser Strand für Kinder **sicher**?
7	Can I ______________ your pen, please?	Kann ich bitte deinen Stift **leihen**?
8	We don't have any camping ______________.	Wir haben keine Camping**ausrüstung**.
9	Can we ______________ some apples from your tree?	Dürfen wir ein paar Äpfel von eurem Baum **pflücken**?
10	Don't ______________ other people's rubbish.	**Heb** nicht den Müll anderer Leute **auf**.
11	When it's cold, I wear ______________.	Wenn es kalt ist, trage ich **Handschuhe**.
12	______________ I visited my aunt.	**Gestern** habe ich meine Tante besucht.

▸ Check

15 What's the word?

Vervollständige die Sätze mit den Wörtern aus dem Kasten.

dark • darkness • safe • safety • silence • silent

1 Don't put your bike here. This isn't a ______________________ place for bikes.

2 I can't read when it's ______________________.

3 At night our flat is ______________________.

4 The village park is great. Children can play there in ______________________.

5 Tom needs absolute ______________________ when he is working.

6 It wasn't easy to find my way in the ______________________.

16 New words and phrases

► SB, p. 25 | VOCABULARY p. 237

1 What does the ______________ over there say?	Was steht auf dem **Schild** da drüben?
2 Five actors came onto the ________________.	Fünf Schauspieler/innen kamen auf die **Bühne**.
3 Sarah has long blond ____________________.	Sarah hat lange blonde **Haare**.
4 Do you play an ____________________?	Spielst du ein **Instrument**?
5 There's a photo of Brighton on the ____________________ of the book.	Auf der **Vorderseite** des Buches ist ein Foto von Brighton.

17 Word partners

Verbinde die Wörter und Ausdrücke, die zusammenpassen.

apartment — wonderful — single — a little — kids

a bit — children — great — flat — one-way

(apartment – flat)

18 Odd word out

Unterstreiche das Wort, das nicht in die Reihe passt.

1 mother – friend – sister – daughter

2 ferry – car – capital – plane

3 hill – river – mountain – campsite

4 silent – quiet – event – loud

5 glove – flag – shoe – hat

6 today – yesterday – tomorrow – year

19 New words and phrases

► SB, p. 26 | VOCABULARY pp. 237–239

1	A trip to another country is a great ____________.	Eine Reise in ein anderes Land ist ein tolles **Abenteuer**.
2	It was dark when we walked ____________ the cinema.	Es war dunkel, als wir **aus** dem Kino **heraus**gingen.
3	Tom was in hospital for the first ____________.	Tom war das erste **Mal** im Krankenhaus.
4	It rained only ____________ when I was in Britain.	Es hat nur **einmal** geregnet, als ich in Großbritannien war.
5	I visit Grandma ____________.	Ich besuche Oma **einmal pro Woche**.
6	Sina thinks that maths is ____________.	Sina findet Mathe **leicht**.
7	How do we ____________ the train station from here?	Wie **kommen** wir von hier **zum** Bahnhof?
8	Can I ____________ your cake?	Kann ich deinen Kuchen **probieren**?
9	It's Tom's birthday tomorrow. He's very ____________.	Tom hat morgen Geburtstag. Er ist sehr **aufgeregt**.
10	Can I come and see you ____________?	Kann ich **heute Nachmittag** zu dir kommen?
11	We ____________ the train in Brighton and ____________ in Southampton.	Wir **sind** in Brighton in den Zug **eingestiegen** und in Southampton **ausgestiegen**.
12	The journey took ____________ two hours.	Die Fahrt dauerte **fast** zwei Stunden.
13	We didn't have to ____________.	Wir mussten nicht **umsteigen**.
14	____________ can't buy tickets on the train.	**Man** kann im Zug keinen Fahrkarten kaufen.
15	The baby is trying to get ____________ the chair.	Das Baby versucht, **auf** den Stuhl zu gelangen.
16	Listen to the ____________ at the station.	Achte auf die **Durchsagen** am Bahnhof.

► Check

20 New words and phrases

▶ SB, pp. 27–28 | VOCABULARY p. 239

1	I think we're walking ________________.	Ich glaube, wir laufen **in die falsche Richtung**.
2	I ________________ that you're feeling better.	Ich **bin froh**, dass du dich wieder besser fühlst.
3	Tom always tries to stay ________________.	Tom versucht immer, **besonnen** zu bleiben.
4	Do you ________________ your friends when you meet?	**Umarmst** du deine Freunde, wenn ihr euch trefft?
5	I don't like ________________ other people.	Ich **umarme** nicht gerne andere Leute.
6	Liam gets a lot of ________________ from his parents.	Liam bekommt viel **Unterstützung** von seinen Eltern.
7	Liam ________________ his parents ________________ him.	Liam **ist** seinen Eltern **dankbar dafür**, dass sie ihn **unterstützen**.
8	Getting lost is a horrible ________________.	Sich zu verlaufen ist ein schreckliches **Gefühl**.
9	We had an ________________ view of the coast from our hotel room.	Wir hatten einen **großartigen** Blick auf die Küste von unserem Hotelzimmer.
10	Can we go into town and ________________ a little?	Können wir in die Stadt fahren und dort ein bisschen **umhergehen**?
11	I ________________ Tom.	Ich **stimme** Tom **zu**.

03

21 Listen carefully!

Höre dir die Sätze aufmerksam an und schreibe das fehlende Wort in die Lücke.

1 Trains from Brighton arrive on ________________ four.

2 Lisa's brother has one ________________, her sister has two ________________.

3 Our school ________________ was great.

4 There are some very good ________________ at our school.

5 You need a lot of ________________ when you go camping.

6 Tom is ________________ about his school trip.

7 They have to ________________ trains in London.

8 Lisa didn't understand the ________________ at the station.

9 She walked the ________________ way.

10 It wasn't easy for her to stay ________________.

22 Secret sentence

Ergänze die fehlenden Buchstaben. Welcher geheime Satz verbirgt sich in diesen Sätzen?

1	Our next holiday **dest**		**nation** is Scotland.
2	Kaya is **b**		**ind**.
3	Can I **borr**		**w** your pen, please?
4	Our **arri**		**al** time is 8.15 p.m.
5	I don't **agr**		**e** with you.
6	Tom's family **st**		**yed** on a campsite in Wales.
7	Mia is a **won**		**erful** sister.
8	Our street is very busy, **e**		**en** at night.
9	Your **fe**		**t** are too big for these shoes.
10	Ari wants to be a **musicia**		.
11	Please buy a **bot**		**le** of milk.
12	Let's go by **undergro**		**nd**.
13	We live in a safe **a**		**ea**.
14	I went inside **wh**		**n** it started to rain.
15	Stop		**creaming**!

The secret sentence is: ______________________________

____

23 New words and phrases

► SB, p. 30 | VOCABULARY pp. 239–240

1	Your text needs a better ____________________.	Dein Text benötigt eine bessere **Struktur**.
2	____________________ in the shop was very expensive.	**Alles** in dem Geschäft war sehr teuer.
3	Our friends visited us at the ____________________ of June.	Unsere Freunde haben uns **Anfang** Juni besucht.
4	Is this you in the ________________ of the photo?	Bist du das in der **Mitte** des Fotos?
5	I can ____________________ my mobile ____________________ my computer.	Ich kann mein Handy mit meinem Computer **verbinden**.
6	He __________________________, but couldn't remember the password.	Er **dachte scharf nach**, konnte sich aber nicht an das Passwort erinnern.
7	It's too cold to play outside. Let's think about an ________________.	Es ist zu kalt, um draußen zu spielen. Lasst uns über eine **Alternative** nachdenken.

► Check

24 Opposites

Finde die Gegenteile.

1 difficult ◄► ____________________

2 boyfriend ◄► ____________________

3 exciting ◄► ____________________

4 into the room ◄► ____________________

5 first ◄► ____________________

6 single ticket ◄► ____________________

7 end ◄► ____________________

8 expensive ◄► ____________________

9 (to) agree ◄► ____________________

25 What's the word?

Vervollständige die Sätze mit den Wörtern aus dem Kasten. Achte dabei auf die Wortart und die richtige Form des Wortes.

experience • hope • hug • link • scream • stay • support • try

1 Mum always gives me a ____________________ when I come home from school.

2 My teachers and my classmates ____________________ me when I was new in class.

3 I ____________________ you're feeling better again.

4 Mrs Evans has twenty years of ____________________ as a doctor.

5 We ____________________ with our cousins in the summer holidays.

6 I was scared when I heard a loud ____________________ in front of our house.

7 I ____________________ lots of different food when we were in Italy.

8 ____________________ the two sentences with 'and'.

26 New words and phrases

► SB, p. 31 | VOCABULARY p. 240

1 What's that ____________________ over there?	Was ist das für ein **Gegenstand** dort drüben?
2 I made a ____________________.	Ich habe einen **Fehler** gemacht.
3 This is your letter. Sorry, I opened it ____________________.	Das ist dein Brief. Entschuldigung, ich habe ihn **aus Versehen** geöffnet.
4 Make a ____________________ of your presentation.	Mache eine **Aufnahme** von deiner Präsentation.
5 Our tour ____________________ a visit to Buckingham Palace.	Unsere Tour **schloss** einen Besuch des Buckingham Palasts **mit ein**.

27 Word search

Finde vierzehn Verben im Buchstabengitter und kreise sie ein. Vervollständige dann die Sätze mit ihnen. Achte auf die Form des Verbs. Suche in diesen Richtungen: ↓ ↑ ← → ↘

1 We ________________ hiking in the mountains last week.

2 We all clapped our hands when the band ________________ to play.

3 Dad ________________ lots of photos when we were on holiday.

4 Mike and Sam ________________ a little sister. She's five.

5 I ________________ the bike with my own money.

6 We went to Italy and ________________ in the sea nearly every day.

7 When Sam was in hospital, Claire ________________ a card for him. She likes drawing.

8 Yesterday I ________________ out lots of pictures for my presentation.

9 ________________ your books on the table, please.

10 ________________ me about your holidays.

11 I don't want to ________________ pizza again today.

12 We ________________ lots of different animals at the zoo yesterday.

13 We ________________ a great time with our grandparents in the summer holidays.

14 I'd like to ________________ to the cinema at the weekend.

S	W	A	M	B	P
B	E	G	A	N	U
G	O	C	D	E	T
T	S	U	E	V	W
E	A	T	G	A	E
L	W	D	A	H	N
L	B	K	O	O	T

28 Different sounds

Welcher Vokallaut klingt anders als die anderen in der Reihe? Unterstreiche das Wort. Suche dann zu jeder Reihe ein passendes Wort im Kasten.

1 bought – call – through – door ________________

2 cake – hard – last – mask ________________

3 eight – plan – stay – wait ________________

4 eye – my – trip – write ________________

5 ghost – old – come – no ________________

6 touch – hug – glove – thought ________________

come • fast • road • taste • thought • time

► Check

29 Let's talk: Über Ferienaktivitäten sprechen

▶ SB, p. 225

Ergänze den Dialog so, dass er für dich stimmt. Die Ausdrücke im Kasten können dir dabei helfen. Du kannst deine Antworten auch aufnehmen und jemanden bitten, sie sich anzuhören und dir Feedback zu geben.

I was at home. • Great, thank you. • We stayed with ... • A bit boring. • Yes, we were. • No, we weren't. • I was in ... with ... • We were ...

Hi, how were your holidays? ________________________________

What did you do in the holidays? ________________________________

____

Were you in a holiday apartment? ________________________________

____

30 Let's talk: Über das Wetter sprechen

▶ SB, p. 225

Schreibe die richtigen Sätze oder Fragen aus dem Kasten in dein Heft.

What was the weather like in Spain? • What's the weather like in Britain in winter? • It's often rainy and cold. • It was hot and sunny.

Unit 2
Friends and heroes

1 New words and phrases

► SB, pp. 46–47 | VOCABULARY p. 241

Lies die Sätze, sieh dir die Bilder an und trage die richtigen Wörter in das Gitter ein.

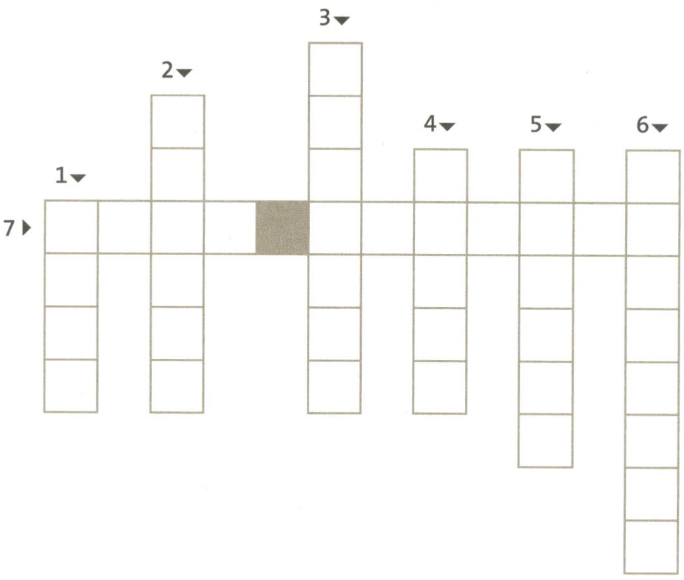

1 My brother is my ???. He is very brave and always there for me.

2 The boy is wearing ???.

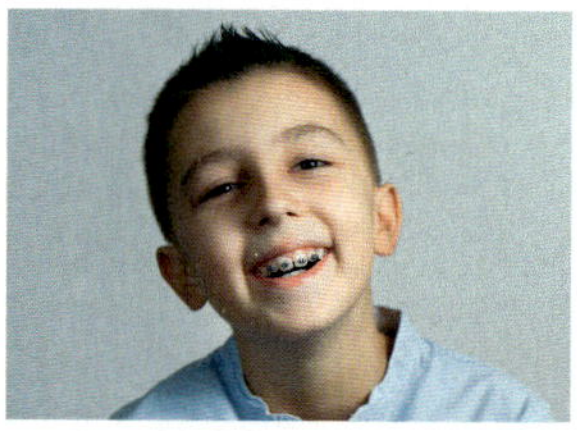

3 The girl is wearing ???.

4 The man has ??? hair.

5 Our neighbours are my ??? too. They help everybody in our street.

6 The woman has long ??? hair.

7 Molly is the perfect ???: She is kind and listens to other students' problems.

► Check

2 New words and phrases

► SB, pp. 48–49 | VOCABULARY pp. 241–242

1	Tom is ______________.	Tom ist **fleißig**.
2	Liam was very quiet when he started school, but now he is a ______________ student.	Liam war sehr still, als er in die Schule kam, aber jetzt ist er ein **selbstsicherer** Schüler.
3	My parents always ______________ tidy my room at the weekend.	Meine Eltern **bringen mich** am Wochenende immer **dazu**, mein Zimmer aufzuräumen.
4	Don't ______________ your little brother when he makes mistakes.	**Lach** nicht **über** deinen kleinen Bruder, wenn er Fehler macht.
5	Horses are ______________ animals.	Pferde sind **starke** Tiere.
6	Tom's father is very ______________.	Toms Vater ist sehr **groß**.
7	Everybody likes ______________ people.	Jeder mag **zuverlässige** Menschen.
8	You must be ______________ with a baby.	Mit einem Baby muss man **geduldig** sein.
9	Our cat is very ______________.	Unsere Katze ist sehr **scheu**.
10	Our dog has a strong ______________.	Unser Hund hat eine starke **Persönlichkeit**.
11	My shelf has the same ______________ as yours.	Mein Regal hat dieselbe **Höhe** wie deines.
12	There are ______________ walls around the park.	Der Park ist von **hohen** Mauern umgeben.
13	How would you describe ______________?	Wie würdest du **dich selbst** beschreiben?
14	Tom's father is an ______________ man.	Toms Vater ist ein **ehrlicher** Mann.

3 New words and phrases

► SB, pp. 50–51 | VOCABULARY pp. 242–243

1	______________ knows where my bike is.	**Niemand** weiß, wo mein Fahrrad ist.
2	You can have the last piece of cake if ______________ wants it.	Du kannst das letzte Stück Kuchen haben, wenn es **niemand sonst** möchte.
3	I often ______________ my grandpa.	Ich **denke** oft **an** meinen Opa.
4	I write with my ______________ hand.	Ich schreibe mit der **rechten** Hand.
5	In Britain, cars must drive ______________.	In Großbritannien müssen Autos **links** fahren.
6	Neil Armstrong was the first man who walked on the ______________.	Neil Armstrong war der erste Mann, der auf dem **Mond** herumgelaufen ist.
7	Sarah often ______________ school events.	Sarah **berichtet** oft **über** Schulveranstaltungen.

4 Bits and pieces

Verbinde die Teile miteinander, um Wörter zu bilden. Achte auf die Schreibung.

your | head | person | reli | hard | confi | no

working | one | able | dent | self | ality | student

5 New words and phrases

► SB, p. 52 | VOCABULARY p. 243

1	Tom ____________ our cat.	Tom **hat** unsere Katze **gerettet**.
2	Do you think that there is ____________ on the moon?	Glaubst du, dass es **Leben** auf dem Mond gibt?
3	People say that cats have seven ____________.	Man sagt, dass Katzen sieben **Leben** haben.
4	____________ is your English teacher?	**Wer** ist dein Englischlehrer?
5	____________ can we ask for help?	**Wen** können wir um Hilfe bitten?
6	____________ did you get the sweets from?	Von **wem** hast du die Süßigkeiten bekommen?
7	How long can you stay ____________?	Wie lange kannst du **unter Wasser** bleiben?
8	I ____________ my left foot.	Ich **habe** mir den linken Fuß **verletzt**.
9	____________ you ____________?	**Bist** du **verletzt**?
10	____________ your dog with me when you go shopping.	**Lass** deinen Hund bei mir, wenn du einkaufen gehst.
11	We ____________ Italy when I was two.	Wir **haben** Italien **verlassen**, als ich zwei war.
12	Please ____________ me ____________.	Bitte **lass** mich **in Ruhe**.

6 New words and phrases

► SB, p. 53 | VOCABULARY p. 243

1	Tom is ____________ in a city. His parents ____________ in the country.	Tom **wächst** in einer Großstadt **auf**. Seine Eltern **sind** auf dem Land **aufgewachsen**.
2	Get ____________ my bed!	Geh **von** meinem Bett **runter**!
3	The baby ____________ the chair.	Das Baby **ist** vom Stuhl **heruntergefallen**.

► Check

7 New words and phrases

▸ SB, pp. 54–55 | VOCABULARY pp. 243–244

1	Lisa is an ______________ who tries to save animals' lives.	Lisa ist eine **Aktivistin**, die versucht Tierleben zu retten.
2	Pete is an ______________. He draws pictures.	Pete ist **Künstler**. Er zeichnet Bilder.
3	What is the ______________ of "tall"?	Was ist das **Gegenteil** von „hoch"?
4	Cara made a ______________ mistake.	Cara hat einen **dummen** Fehler gemacht.
5	Sometimes I'm too ______________ to do my homework.	Manchmal bin ich zu **faul**, meine Hausaufgaben zu machen.
6	Dilek ______________ a lot of time ______________ her cousins.	Dilek **verbringt** viel Zeit **mit** ihren Cousinen.
7	As a student, Sam ______________ a lot of money ______________ computer games.	Als Schüler **hat** Sam viel Geld **für** Computerspiele **ausgegeben**.
8	I'm trying to think ______________ today.	Ich versuche heute **positiv** zu denken.
9	Tim's brother is a ______________ and his sister wants to become a ______________ too.	Tims Bruder ist **Arzt** und seine Schwester möchte auch **Ärztin** werden.
10	Kim wants to be a ______________.	Kim möchte **Krankenpfleger** werden.
11	Sarah had a car ______________.	Sarah hatte einen Auto**unfall**.

04

8 Listen carefully!

Höre dir die Sätze aufmerksam an und schreibe das fehlende Wort in die Lücke.

1 Lucy has long brown ______________.

2 Liam can't see without his ______________.

3 Adam has ______________ on his teeth.

4 Why are you ______________?

5 I'm ______________ money for a new bike.

6 Please don't ______________ the door open.

7 Kerry and Dan got ______________ in June.

8 Dan ______________ up in Ireland.

9 What's the ______________ of "big"?

10 Jim fell ______________ his bike and hurt his left foot.

9 New words and phrases

▸ SB, p. 56 | VOCABULARY pp. 244–245

1 Luca _______________ in London.	Luca **ist** in London **geboren**.
2 How many people live on _______________?	Wie viele Menschen leben auf der **Erde**?
3 Sean wants to _______________ a teacher.	Sean möchte Lehrer **werden**.
4 The wind had so much _______________ that I couldn't walk home.	Der Wind hatte so viel **Kraft**, dass ich nicht zu Fuß nach Hause gehen konnte.

10 Lost words

Füge das richtige Wort aus den Luftballons in die Sätze ein.

1 Zoe spends a lot of money ___on___ sweets.

2 I'd like to spend more time _________ my friends.

3 When I was a kid, everybody laughed _________ my red hair.

4 Where did you grow _________?

5 Luca fell _________ the wall and hurt his head.

6 Sam's brother was born _________ 2018.

7 Is there life _________ Mars?

8 Molly shares a room with her sister. Her bed is _________ the left.

9 Sam often thinks _________ his grandpa. He really likes him.

11 Scrambled words

Hier sind einige Buchstaben durcheinandergeraten. Schreibe die Wörter richtig auf.

1 Liam is a very *nficontde* student. _______________

2 Molly took lots of *terderunwa* photos on holiday. _______________

3 As an *iviactst* John fights for animal rights. _______________

4 The *poitopse* of "big" is "small". _______________

5 Jim wants to *mebcoe* a vet when he grows up. _______________

6 Rob was hurt in an *ntciacde*. _______________

7 John's grandpa was an *tiasrt*. _______________

8 Say something *vesipoti* about yourself. _______________

9 "Men can't cook" is a *ptisud* thing to say. _______________

▸ Check

12 New words and phrases

▸ SB, pp. 57–58 | VOCABULARY pp. 245–246

1	Our ________________ is the earth.	Unser **Planet** ist die Erde.
2	The cinema isn't ________________ from here.	Das Kino ist nicht **weit** von hier **entfernt**.
3	We can take ________________ bus from here.	Wir können **jeden** Bus von hier nehmen.
4	Do you have ________________ questions?	Hast du **irgendwelche** Fragen?
5	We ________________ the trees in our town.	Wir **kämpfen für** die Bäume in unserer Stadt.
6	Please bring a ________________ bottle, not a plastic bottle.	Bitte bring eine **Metall**flasche und keine Plastikflasche mit.
7	Which part of your ________________ hurts?	Welcher Teil deines **Körpers** tut dir weh?
8	Never cycle without a ________________!	Fahr nie ohne **Helm** Rad!
9	Would you eat cat food ________________?	Würdest du Katzenfutter **als Mutprobe** essen?
10	Horses have four ________________.	Pferde haben vier **Beine**.
11	Drawing a ________________ is difficult.	Eine **Nase** zu zeichnen ist schwierig.
12	Our dog ________________ our car ________________ its sound.	Unser Hund **erkennt** unser Auto **am** Klang.
13	Rob would like to swim with ________________.	Rob würde gern mit **Delfinen** schwimmen.
14	Tarek is a really nice ________________.	Tarek ist ein wirklich netter **Typ**.
15	Don't use ________________ near children.	Benutze keine **Chemikalien** in der Nähe von Kindern.
16	Snakes live in the water and on ________________.	Schlangen leben im Wasser und an **Land**.
17	What's your ________________ school day like?	Wie sieht dein **normaler** Schultag aus?
18	Please call the ________________.	Bitte rufen Sie die **Polizei**.
19	Ron plays the ________________ in the school drama.	Ron spielt den **Schurken** im Schultheaterstück.
20	Our dog has a white and a brown ________________.	Unser Hund hat ein weißes und ein braunes **Ohr**.
21	Bring your ________________.	Bring deinen **Badeanzug** mit.
22	Let's ________________ the tree over there.	Lass uns **auf** den Baum dort **klettern**.
23	Sam's cat doesn't ________________ mice.	Sams Katze **tötet** keine Mäuse.
24	In summer I often wear ________________.	Im Sommer trage ich oft **Kleider**.
25	Sometimes I'd like to be ________________.	Manchmal möchte ich **unsichtbar** sein.
26	Umbrellas ________________ you ________________ the rain.	Schirme **beschützen** einen **vor** dem Regen.

13 New words and phrases

► SB, p. 59 | VOCABULARY pp. 247–248

1	We were very sad when our dog ________.	Wir waren sehr traurig, als unser Hund **starb**.
2	What ________ he ________?	**Woran ist** er **gestorben**?
3	There's a ________ seagull on the beach.	Da liegt eine **tote** Möwe am Strand.
4	Tom is a very ________ artist.	Tom ist ein sehr **kreativer** Künstler.
5	In Germany every child has the ________ to go to school.	In Deutschland hat jedes Kind das **Recht**, zur Schule zu gehen.
6	Ms Hall is our new ________.	Frau Hall ist unsere neue **Schulleiterin**.
7	Lara is ________ new technology.	Lara ist **an** neuer Technologie **interessiert**.
8	Some activists are fighting ________ a new road through our town forest.	Einige Aktivisten kämpfen **gegen** eine neue Straße durch unseren Stadtwald.
9	Ron and Rick have the same ________.	Ron und Rick haben dieselbe **Krankheit**.
10	Walt Disney has won lots of ________.	Walt Disney hat viele **Preise** gewonnen.
11	Are you interested in ________?	Interessierst du dich für **Philosphie**?
12	What's the best place ________ for you?	Was ist der beste Platz **auf der Welt** für dich?
13	Sina's grandpa fought in two ________.	Sinas Opa hat in zwei **Weltkriegen** gekämpft.
14	Don't talk ________ the concert.	Sprich nicht **während** des Konzerts.
15	Most people want to live in ________.	Die meisten Menschen wollen in **Frieden** leben.
16	Great Britain is ________ fish and chips.	Großbritannien ist **für** Fisch und Pommes frites **berühmt**.
17	We need a new coffee ________.	Wir brauchen eine neue Kaffee**maschine**.
18	Can you ________ my new phone?	Kannst du mein neues Handy **programmieren**?
19	"________ shoes are these?" – "Mick's."	„**Wessen** Schuhe sind das?" – „Micks."

14 New words and phrases

► SB, p. 60 | VOCABULARY p. 248

1	Please call an ________.	Bitte rufe einen **Krankenwagen**.
2	Yesterday Molly ________ off her bike.	Gestern **ist** Molly von ihrem Rad **gefallen**.
3	Don't ________ on the sofa.	**Spring** nicht auf dem Sofa.
4	There are no shops on this ________ of the street.	Auf dieser Straßen**seite** gibt es keine Geschäfte.

► Check

15 New words and phrases

► SB, pp. 61–62 | VOCABULARY pp. 248–250

1	Lions are ______ animals.	Löwen sind **gefährliche** Tiere.
2	I was ______ when my brother had a car accident.	Ich war **schockiert**, als mein Bruder einen Autounfall hatte.
3	Sarah's ______ still hurts.	Sarahs **Knöchel** schmerzt noch immer.
4	The ball ______ me in the face.	Der Ball **traf** mich im Gesicht.
5	I sleep on my ______.	Ich schlafe auf dem **Rücken**.
6	If you like the book, you can ______ it.	Wenn dir das Buch gefällt, kannst du es **behalten**.
7	The children were tired and ______ ______ in the car.	Die Kinder waren müde und **schliefen** im Auto **ein**.
8	______ before you start to sing.	**Atme ein**, bevor du anfängst zu singen.
9	I'm cold. I need another ______.	Mir ist kalt. Ich brauche eine weitere **Decke**.
10	Liam's uncle likes telling ______.	Liams Onkel erzählt gerne **Witze**.
11	Something fell on my ______.	Etwas ist mir auf den **Nacken** gefallen.
12	Molly was very ______ when some children laughed at her.	Molly war sehr **aufgebracht**, als ein paar Kinder sie auslachten.
13	Mum never ______ me to school.	Mama **fährt** mich nie zur Schule.
14	Our village got a new ______.	Unser Dorf hat ein neues **Feuerwehrauto** bekommen.
15	Lisa's phone is ______.	Lisas Handy ist **kaputt**.
16	It's important that parents ______ their ______.	Es ist wichtig, dass Eltern ihre **Versprechen halten**.

16 The fourth word

Ergänze das fehlende Wort.

1 see – eye → hear – ______

2 sun – day → moon – ______

3 helmet – head → boots – ______

4 accident – ambulance → fire – ______

5 up – down → right – ______

► Check

17 What's the word?

Vervollständige die Sätze mit den Wörtern aus dem Kasten. Achte dabei auf die Wortart und die richtige Form des Wortes.

climb • dare • dress • fight • joke • jump • land • laugh • promise • shock

1 My brother ______________________ me an ice cream because I did his homework for him.

2 I like your blue ______________________!

3 Our plane ______________________ ten minutes late.

4 Please don't ______________________ on my bed. It isn't a trampoline.

5 We ______________________ three mountains in the summer holidays.

6 Some of Ken's ______________________ aren't funny at all.

7 Who started this stupid ______________________?

8 Nothing really ______________________ our parents. They're very cool.

9 I like my friend because he always makes me ______________________.

10 Sam climbed a high tree for a ______________________.

18 New words and phrases

► SB, p. 64 | VOCABULARY p. 250

1 Let's ______________ how we can go to the coast by train.	Lasst uns **herausfinden**, wie wir mit dem Zug an die Küste fahren können.
2 Tom showed great ______________ when he saved the dog.	Tom hat großen **Mut** gezeigt, als er den Hund gerettet hat.
3 You can't buy ______________.	**Glück** kann man nicht kaufen.
4 The English word "menu" is a ______________ ______________. It looks like the German word "Menü", but it means "Speisekarte".	Das englische Wort „menu" ist ein **„falscher Freund"**. Es sieht aus wie das deutsche Wort „Menü", bedeutet aber „Speisekarte".

19 Opposites

Finde die Gegenteile.

1 far ◄► ______________

2 lazy ◄► ______________

3 happiness ◄► ______________

4 against ◄► ______________

5 positive ◄► ______________

6 tall ◄► ______________

7 patient ◄► ______________

8 shy ◄► ______________

► Check

20 New words and phrases

► SB, p. 65 | VOCABULARY pp. 250–251

1	Marie Curie was a great ________________.	Marie Curie war eine großartige **Wissenschaftlerin**.
2	A ________________ talks to important or interesting people on TV or on the radio.	Ein/e **Moderator/in** spricht im Fernsehen oder Radio mit wichtigen oder interessanten Leuten.
3	Who is your favourite ________________?	Wer ist dein/e Lieblings**sportler/in**?
4	Some ________________ make a lot of money.	Einige **Sportler/innen** verdienen sehr viel Geld.
5	It's a ________________ that lots of African children can't go to school.	Es ist eine **Tatsache**, dass viele afrikanische Kinder nicht zur Schule gehen können.
6	When Columbus ________________ America, he thought he was in India.	Als Kolumbus Amerika **entdeckte**, dachte er, er sei in Indien.
7	Well done! All your answers are ____________.	Gut gemacht! Deine Antworten sind alle **korrekt**.
8	It takes ________________ two hours to go from Brighton to London by car.	Es dauert **mindestens** zwei Stunden, um mit dem Auto von Brighton nach London zu fahren.
9	"Is Tom coming to the party?" – "________________________________."	„Kommt Tom auf die Party?" – „**Ich glaube ja.**"

21 Listen carefully!

05

Höre dir die Sätze aufmerksam an und schreibe das fehlende Wort in die Lücke.

1 When we go hiking in the mountains, I wear ________________________.

2 ________________________ are usually very friendly.

3 We had a car ________________________ last week, but nobody was hurt.

4 We didn't need an ________________________.

5 Boris fell off his bike and hurt his ________________________.

6 Mina wants to become a ________________________.

7 I need a new ________________________.

8 You have to be careful when you work with ________________________.

9 Call 999 for a ________________________!

10 These roads are ________________________ for children.

22 What did they do?

Vervollständige die Sätze mit den Verben in Klammern. Verwende *simple past*.

1 Tom's parents ________________ (give) him a bike for his birthday.

2 Mum always wanted to be a teacher, but in the end she ________________ (become) a scientist.

3 We ________________ (leave) our dog with our neighbours when we went to Italy.

4 Molly ________________ (spend) a lot of time with her grandparents when she was little.

5 We were happy when we ________________ (find) a nice house.

6 Tim ________________ (feel) ill, so Luke ________________ (drive) Daria to school.

7 Our team ________________ (fight) hard and won[1] the game.

8 We ________________ (wait) at the bus stop, but the bus never ________________ (come).

[1] (to) **win, won, won**

23 Different sounds

Welcher Vokallaut klingt anders als die anderen in der Reihe? Unterstreiche das Wort. Suche dann zu jeder Reihe zwei passende Wörter im Kasten.

art • came • climb • day • drive • far • girl • hurt • their • weird • where • year

1 hair – wear – her – dare ____________

2 straight – hard – save – change ____________

3 first – earth – work – shock ____________

4 learn – here – ear – hear ____________

5 side – buy – blind – kill ____________

6 laugh – arm – land – mask ____________

24 Let's talk: Sich und andere beschreiben

► SB, p. 223

Sieh dir das Bild an und beschreibe die beiden Personen so exakt und ausführlich wie möglich. Die Wörter im Kasten helfen dir. Du kannst deine Beschreibung auch aufnehmen und jemanden bitten, sie sich anzuhören und dir Feedback zu geben.

blond • black • computers • curly • drawing • good at/with • hair • I think that • kind • (to) look • on the left/right • short • straight • tall

► Check

Unit 3
Activities and games

1 New words and phrases

► SB, pp. 78–79 | VOCABULARY pp. 251–252

1	In summer we always enjoy the __________ of Grandma's garden.	Im Sommer genießen wir immer die **Schönheit** von Omas Garten.
2	Our neighbour's dog is a big __________.	Der Hund unserer Nachbarn ist eine große **Bestie**.
3	Our playground is always __________ children.	Unser Spielplatz ist immer **voller** Kinder.
4	I like the __________ best.	Ich mag die **Seilrutsche** am liebsten.
5	A new job is often a __________.	Eine neue Stelle ist oft eine **Herausforderung**.
6	Last year Phil __________ __________ of a new job far away from home.	Letztes Jahr **hat sich** Phil der **Herausforderung** eines neuen Jobs weit weg von zu Hause **gestellt**.
7	Mara is taking __________ Spanish class.	Mara besucht **einen zweistündigen** Spanischkurs.
8	__________ are important animals.	**Insekten** sind wichtige Tiere.
9	Let's __________ a hotel room in London.	Lass uns ein Hotelzimmer in London **buchen**.
10	What'__________ at the cinema this evening?	Was **läuft** heute Abend im Kino?
11	Zola is a __________ girl. She sings and plays the guitar.	Zola ist ein **musikalisches** Mädchen. Sie singt und spielt Gitarre.
12	Who is your favourite __________?	Wer ist dein/e Lieblings**schauspieler/in**?
13	I always book a __________ on the train.	Ich buche mir immer einen **Sitzplatz** im Zug.
14	Please __________.	Bitte **nehmen Sie Platz**.

2 What's the right word?

beautiful • challenging • musical • sit • three-week

Vervollständige die Sätze mit den Wörtern aus dem Kasten.

1 A __________ holiday in Spain sounds great!
2 'The Lion King' is a very popular __________.
3 What a __________ day! Let's go swimming.
4 Teaching 14-year-old students can be quite __________.
5 You can __________ with me if you like.

3 New words and phrases

► SB, p. 80 | VOCABULARY pp. 252–253

1	Luke likes scary places like ________________.	Luke mag gruselige Orte wie zum Beispiel **Kerker**.
2	Mara likes drawing ________________.	Mara zeichnet gern **Drachen**.
3	We often ________________ things in our English lessons.	Wir **stellen** oft Dinge **in einem Rollenspiel** im Englischunterricht **dar**.
4	Who ________________ your football team?	Wer **trainiert** eure Fußballmannschaft?
5	Lara is a ________________ dancer.	Lara ist **Profi**tänzerin.
6	We visited Edinburgh ________________ when we were in Scotland.	Wir haben uns die **Burg** in Edinburgh angesehen, als wir in Schottland waren. 
7	Can you ________________?	Kannst du **stricken**?
8	Molly took a German ________________.	Molly hat einen Deutsch**kurs** besucht.
9	Molly must ________________ the German test next week.	Molly muss sich **auf** den Deutschtest nächste Woche **vorbereiten**.
10	Students who like ________________ can choose drama at our school.	Schüler/innen, die gern **Theater spielen**, können Darstellendes Spiel an unserer Schule wählen.
11	If a child falls into the water, you must ________________ fast to save them.	Wenn ein Kind ins Wasser fällt, muss man schnell **handeln**, um es zu retten.
12	Are you looking for a new hobby? What about ________________?	Suchst du ein neues Hobby? Wie wäre es mit **Fotografie**?
13	Mara is a ________________ person. She plays football and is a good swimmer.	Mara ist eine **sportliche** Person. Sie spielt Fußball und ist eine gute Schwimmerin.
14	The summer concerts always ________________ ________________ in June.	Die Sommerkonzerte **finden** immer im Juni **statt**.

► Check

4 New words and phrases

► SB, pp. 81–83 | VOCABULARY pp. 253–254

1	"We'______________ hike in the mountains." – "What ______________ you ______________ at the weekend?"	„Wir **haben vor**, in den Bergen zu wandern." „Was **habt** ihr am Wochenende vor?"
2	My new phone has a good ______________.	Mein neues Handy hat eine gute **Kamera**.
3	There's a good film on ______________.	**Heute Abend** gibt es einen guten Film.
4	Tom has a ______________ with Lara on Sunday.	Tom hat eine **Verabredung** mit Lara am Sonntag.
5	Jim lives ______________ in London.	Jim wohnt **irgendwo** in London.

5 Bits and pieces

Verbinde die Teile miteinander, um Wörter zu bilden. Achte auf die korrekte Schreibung.

zip chal role in mu cam to dun

play geon era night sect wire sical lenge

6 What's the right word?

Vervollständige die Sätze mit den Wörtern aus dem Kasten.

beauty • castle • full of • seat • somewhere • two-hour

1 My shoes are ____________________ water.
2 We went on a ____________________ ghost tour.
3 Please take a ____________________.
4 I'd like to go ____________________ warm.
5 Your dog is a ____________________.
6 The ____________________ is open to visitors on Wednesdays and Sundays.

7 New words and phrases

► SB, p. 84 | VOCABULARY p. 254

1	My parents often go to ______________ concerts.	Meine Eltern gehen oft in **klassische** Konzerte.
2	Tim plays ______________ guitar.	Tim spielt **akustische** Gitarre.

8 New words and phrases

▸ SB, p. 85 | VOCABULARY p. 254

1	Tom is older ____________ Tarek.	Tom ist älter **als** Tarek.
2	"I'd like two of these cakes." – "I'm sorry, this is ____________."	„Ich möchte zwei von diesen Kuchen." – „Tut mir leid, das ist **der letzte**."
3	Lara has two dogs, a ____________ and a ____________.	Lara hat zwei Hunde, einen **großen** und einen **kleinen**.
4	I need five pens, two ____________, two ____________ and a ____________.	Ich benötige fünf Stifte: zwei **grüne**, zwei **rote** und einen **gelben**.
5	Do you have the ____________ of this song?	Hast du den **Liedtext** zu diesem Song?
6	Tarek is a very ____________ boy. He has lots of ____________.	Tarek ist ein sehr **aktiver** Junge. Er hat viel **Energie**.
7	The weather was already bad when we arrived and then got ____________ every day.	Das Wetter war schon schlecht, als wir ankamen, und wurde dann jeden Tag **schlechter**.
8	I'm hoping for ____________ weather next week.	Ich hoffe auf **besseres** Wetter nächste Woche.
9	Toni's pizzas are good, but not ____________ ____________ Toto's.	Tonis Pizzas sind gut, aber nicht **so gut wie** Totos.
10	____________ your ideas ____________ your partner's ideas.	**Vergleiche** deine Ideen **mit** denen deines Partners / deiner Partnerin.

9 Listen carefully!

06

Höre dir die Sätze aufmerksam an und schreibe das fehlende Wort in die Lücke.

1 Learning a new language can be very ____________.

2 Sam must ____________ for the Spanish test.

3 Cem's favourite hobby is ____________.

4 He bought a new ____________ online.

5 Liz is very ____________.

6 Tyler wants to become an ____________.

7 Tom's uncle is a ____________ dancer.

8 We saw lots of ____________ in Scotland.

9 Cem and Liz have a ____________.

10 They're going to meet online ____________.

▸ Check

10 What's the word?

Vervollständige die Sätze mit den Wörtern aus dem Kasten. Achte auf die richtige Form.

(to) book • booking • (to) prepare • preparation • seat • (to) sit • (to) train • trainer

1 Please take a ______________.
2 Sam is a fitness ______________.
3 Lara has a ______________ for 'The Lion King'.
4 Can you ______________ dinner now, please?
5 Joel ______________ horses.
6 We ______________ a two-week holiday in Italy last night.
7 You don't need much ______________ time for this dish.
8 The weather is great. Let's ______________ outside.

11 New words and phrases

► SB, p. 86 | VOCABULARY p. 254

1 Do you watch ______________ films?	Guckst du dir **Sciencefiction**-Filme an?
2 How would you ______________ this film?	Wie würdest du diesen Film **bewerten**?
3 Do you look at the ______________ before you buy something on the internet?	Schaust du dir die **Bewertungen** an, bevor du etwas im Internet kaufst?
4 Too much sugar has a bad ______________ ______________ your teeth.	Zu viel Zucker hat eine schlechte **Auswirkung auf** deine Zähne.
5 The ______________ in this film are amazing.	Die **Spezialeffekte** in diesem Film sind großartig.
6 What was your ______________ holiday experience?	Was war dein **schlimmstes** Ferienerlebnis?
7 And what was your ______________ holiday experience?	Und was war dein **bestes** Ferienerlebnis?
8 All my bookshelves are full. I have no ______________ for books any more.	Alle meine Bücherregale sind voll. Ich habe keinen **Platz** mehr für Bücher.

12 New words and phrases

► SB, p. 87 | VOCABULARY p. 255

1 Films with ______________ can be scary.	Filme mit **Außerirdischen** können unheimlich sein.
2 Do you read books or ______________?	Liest du Bücher oder **Zeitschriften**?

13 What's the word: *one* or *ones*?

Vervollständige die Sätze mit den richtigen Wörtern.

1 "I like the T-shirt." – "Which ______________?
The red ______________ or the green ______________?" –
"The green ______________."

2 Mario has four cats, two brown ______________ and two black ______________. One of the black ______________ is quite old.

3 Luke needs some new trousers. His old ______________ are too small.

14 New words and phrases

► SB, p. 88 | VOCABULARY p. 255

1	Your toy cat looks very ______________.	Deine Spielzeugkatze sieht sehr **echt** aus.
2	We often go walking in a ______________ near our village.	Wir gehen oft in einem **Wald** in der Nähe unseres Dorfes spazieren.
3	There's a ______________ over the river.	Es gibt eine **Brücke** über den Fluss.
4	Tom lives on the third floor and has to climb lots of ______________ every day.	Tom wohnt im dritten Stock und muss täglich viele **Treppen** steigen.
5	I can't find my ______________.	Ich finde meinen **Schlüssel** nicht.
6	I often ask my brother not to sing in my room, but he ______________ it.	Ich bitte meinen Bruder oft, nicht in meinem Zimmer zu singen, aber er **tut** es **immer wieder**.
7	______________ at the book shop. Walk to the cinema and ______________ there.	**Bieg** am Buchladen **rechts ab**. Geh bis zum Kino und **bieg** dort **links ab**.
8	Walk ______________ until you get to the school.	Geh **geradeaus weiter**, bis du zur Schule gelangst.
9	Walk ______________ theatre and then turn right.	Geh **am** Theater **vorbei** und bieg dann rechts ab.
10	Let's walk ______________ the bridge.	Lass uns **über** die Brücke gehen.

► Check

ADVANCED lighthouse 2

Wordmaster

Lösungen

Cornelsen

Hello again! The last days of the holidays

1 New words and phrases

▸ SB; pp. 10–11 | VOCABULARY p. 232

1 last • **2** tomorrow • **3** look for • **4** wait for • **5** sleep late; slept late

2 Listen carefully!

1 tastes • **2** last • **3** tomorrow • **4** ice cream • **5** looking for • **6** wait for • **7** slept late • **8** sleep late

Unit 1: Travel and holidays

1 New words and phrases

▸ SB, pp. 12–13 | VOCABULARY pp. 232–233

1 I was • **2** trip • **3** We were • **4** I wasn't / I was not • **5** We weren't / We were not • **6** capital (city) • **7** mountain • **8** campsite • **9** apartment • **10** a bit

2 New words and phrases

▸ SB, p. 14 | VOCABULARY p. 233

1 stays • **2** sunbathe • **3** mother; father • **4** foot • **5** feet

3 New words and phrases

▸ SB, p. 15 | VOCABULARY p. 233

1 grandparents • **2** ferry • **3** plane • **4** hill • **5** river • **6** by the river

4 New words and phrases

▸ SB, p. 16 | VOCABULARY p. 234

1 sort of • **2** all sorts of • **3** scary • **4** when • **5** ghost • **6** dark • **7** vampires • **8** costumes • **9** underground • **10** A long time ago • **11** screams • **12** touch • **13** out

5 Word snake

1 capital • **2** plane • **3** trip • **4** costume • **5** apartment • **6** campsite

6 What's the word: *was* or *were*?

1 were • **2** Were • **3** weren't; were • **4** Was • **5** was; wasn't

7 Lost words

1 for • **2** of • **3** by • **4** with • **5** in • **6** on • **7** at • **8** for • **9** in • **10** by • **11** on • **12** with

8 New words and phrases

▸ SB, p. 17 | VOCABULARY pp. 234–235

1 past • **2** blind • **3** through • **4** mask • **5** eyes • **6** put my hands out • **7** experience • **8** Transport • **9** relax

9 New words and phrases

▸ SB, p. 18 | VOCABULARY p. 235

1 hope • **2** pride; proud • **3** event • **4** thousand • **5** arrival • **6** platform

10 New words and phrases

► SB, p. 19 | VOCABULARY p. 235

1 destination • 2 single / one-way ticket • 3 return (ticket) • 4 cheap

11 New words and phrases

► SB, pp. 20–21 | VOCABULARY p. 236

1 didn't go / did not go • 2 flags • 3 cannot/can't; anything • 4 cannot/can't; at all • 5 rainbow • 6 even • 7 girlfriend • 8 boyfriend • 9 area • 10 child; children • 11 concert • 12 musician • 13 wonderful • 14 piano

12 Listen carefully!

1 mountains • 2 ferry • 3 sunbathing • 4 ghost • 5 vampires • 6 touch • 7 dark • 8 through • 9 experience • 10 eyes

13 Letter code

1 a • 2 e • 3 o • 4 n

14 New words and phrases

► SB, pp. 23–24 | VOCABULARY pp. 236–237

1 to make friends • 2 sights • 3 tower; Tower • 4 silent • 5 Plastic bottles • 6 safe • 7 borrow • 8 equipment • 9 pick • 10 pick up • 11 gloves • 12 Yesterday

15 What's the word?

1 safe • 2 dark • 3 silent • 4 safety • 5 silence • 6 darkness

16 New words and phrases

► SB, p. 25 | VOCABULARY p. 237

1 sign • 2 stage • 3 hair • 4 instrument • 5 front

17 Word partners

1 apartment – flat • 2 wonderful – great • 3 single – one-way • 4 a little – a bit • 5 kids – children

18 Odd word out

1 friend • 2 capital • 3 campsite • 4 event • 5 flag • 6 year

19 New words and phrases

► SB, p. 26 | VOCABULARY pp. 237–239

1 adventure • 2 out of • 3 time • 4 once • 5 once a week • 6 easy • 7 get to • 8 try • 9 excited • 10 this afternoon • 11 got on; got off • 12 nearly • 13 change (trains) • 14 You • 15 onto • 16 announcements

20 New words and phrases

► SB, pp. 27–28 | VOCABULARY p. 239

1 the wrong way • 2 am/'m glad • 3 calm • 4 hug • 5 hugging • 6 support • 7 is grateful to; for supporting • 8 feeling • 9 awesome • 10 walk around • 11 agree with

21 Listen carefully!

1 platform • **2** child; children • **3** concert • **4** musicians • **5** equipment • **6** excited • **7** change • **8** announcements • **9** wrong • **10** calm

22 Secret sentence

1 destination • **2** blind • **3** borrow • **4** arrival • **5** agree • **6** stayed • **7** wonderful • **8** even • **9** feet • **10** musician • **11** bottle • **12** underground • **13** area • **14** when • **15** screaming

Secret sentence: I love adventures.

23 New words and phrases

► SB, p. 30 | VOCABULARY pp. 239–240

1 structure • **2** Everything • **3** beginning • **4** middle • **5** link; to/with • **6** thought hard • **7** alternative

24 Opposites

1 easy • **2** girlfriend • **3** boring • **4** out of the room • **5** last • **6** return (ticket) • **7** beginning • **8** cheap • **9** (to) disagree

25 What's the word?

1 hug • **2** supported • **3** hope • **4** experience • **5** stayed • **6** scream • **7** tried • **8** Link

26 New words and phrases

► SB, p. 31 | VOCABULARY p. 240

1 object • **2** mistake • **3** by mistake • **4** recording • **5** included

27 Word search

1 went • **2** began • **3** took • **4** have • **5** bought • **6** swam • **7** made • **8** cut • **9** Put • **10** Tell • **11** eat • **12** saw • **13** had • **14** go

28 Different sounds

1 through; thought • **2** cake; fast • **3** plan; taste • **4** trip; time • **5** come; road • **6** thought; come

29 Let's talk: Über Ferienaktivitäten sprechen

► SB, p. 225

(*Lösungsbeispiel*)

Great, thank you. / A bit boring.

I was at home. / I was in *[dein Urlaubsort]* with my family / my parents / friends / ...

Yes, we were. / No, we weren't. We were on a campsite. / We stayed with friends. / We stayed with my grandparents.

30 Let's talk: Über das Wetter sprechen

► SB, p. 225

1 What was the weather like in Spain? – It was hot and sunny.

2 What's the weather like in Britain in winter? – It's often rainy and cold.

Unit 2: Friends and heroes

1 New words and phrases

▸ SB, pp. 46–47 | VOCABULARY p. 241

1 hero • 2 braces • 3 glasses • 4 curly • 5 heroes • 6 straight • 7 head student

2 New words and phrases

▸ SB, pp. 48–49 | VOCABULARY pp. 241–242

1 hard-working • 2 confident • 3 make me • 4 laugh at • 5 strong • 6 tall • 7 reliable • 8 patient • 9 shy • 10 personality • 11 height • 12 high • 13 yourself • 14 honest

3 New words and phrases

▸ SB, pp. 50–51 | VOCABULARY pp. 242–243

1 No one / Nobody • 2 no one else • 3 think of • 4 right • 5 on the left • 6 moon • 7 reports on

4 Bits and pieces

1 yourself • 2 head student • 3 personality • 4 reliable • 5 hard-working • 6 confident • 7 no one

5 New words and phrases

▸ SB, p. 52 | VOCABULARY p. 243

1 saved • 2 life • 3 lives • 4 Who • 5 Who • 6 Who • 7 underwater • 8 hurt • 9 Are; hurt • 10 Leave • 11 left • 12 leave; alone

6 New words and phrases

▸ SB, p. 53 | VOCABULARY p. 243

1 growing up; grew up • 2 off • 3 fell off

7 New words and phrases

▸ SB, pp. 54–55 | VOCABULARY pp. 243–244

1 activist • 2 artist • 3 opposite • 4 stupid • 5 lazy • 6 spends; with • 7 spent; on • 8 positive • 9 doctor; doctor • 10 nurse • 11 accident

8 Listen carefully!

1 hair • 2 glasses • 3 braces • 4 laughing • 5 saving • 6 leave • 7 married • 8 grew • 9 opposite • 10 off

9 New words and phrases

▸ SB, p. 56 | VOCABULARY pp. 244–245

1 was born • 2 earth • 3 become • 4 power

10 Lost words

1 on • 2 with • 3 at • 4 up • 5 off • 6 in • 7 on • 8 on • 9 of

11 Scrambled words

1 confident • **2** underwater • **3** activist • **4** opposite • **5** become • **6** accident • **7** artist • **8** positive • **9** stupid

12 New words and phrases

► SB, pp. 57–58 | VOCABULARY pp. 245–246

1 planet • **2** far • **3** any • **4** any • **5** fight for • **6** metal • **7** body • **8** helmet • **9** for a dare • **10** legs • **11** nose • **12** knows; by • **13** dolphins • **14** guy • **15** chemicals • **16** land • **17** normal • **18** police • **19** villain • **20** ear • **21** swimsuit • **22** climb • **23** kill • **24** dresses • **25** invisible • **26** protect; from

13 New words and phrases

► SB, p. 59 | VOCABULARY pp. 247–248

1 died • **2** did; die of • **3** dead • **4** creative • **5** right • **6** head teacher • **7** interested in • **8** against • **9** disease • **10** awards • **11** philosophy • **12** in the world • **13** world wars • **14** during • **15** peace • **16** famous for • **17** machine • **18** program • **19** Whose

14 New words and phrases

► SB, p. 60 | VOCABULARY p. 248

1 ambulance • **2** fell • **3** jump • **4** side

15 New words and phrases

► SB, pp. 61–62 | VOCABULARY pp. 248–250

1 dangerous • **2** shocked • **3** ankle • **4** hit • **5** back • **6** keep • **7** fell asleep • **8** Breathe in • **9** blanket • **10** jokes • **11** neck • **12** upset • **13** drives • **14** fire engine • **15** broken • **16** keep; promises

16 The fourth word

1 ear • **2** night • **3** feet • **4** fire engine • **5** left

17 What's the word?

1 promised • **2** dress • **3** landed • **4** jump • **5** climbed • **6** jokes • **7** fight • **8** shocks • **9** laugh • **10** dare

18 New words and phrases

► SB, p. 64 | VOCABULARY p. 250

1 work out • **2** bravery • **3** happiness • **4** false friend

19 Opposites

1 near • **2** hard-working • **3** unhappiness/sadness • **4** for • **5** negative • **6** short • **7** impatient • **8** confident

20 New words and phrases

► SB, p. 65 | VOCABULARY pp. 250–251

1 scientist • **2** presenter • **3** sportsperson • **4** sportspeople • **5** fact • **6** discovered • **7** correct • **8** at least • **9** I think so.

21 Listen carefully!

1 walking boots • **2** Dolphins • **3** accident • **4** ambulance • **5** ankle • **6** scientist • **7** swimsuit • **8** chemicals • **9** fire engine • **10** dangerous

22 What did they do?

1 gave • **2** became • **3** left • **4** spent • **5** found • **6** felt; drove • **7** fought • **8** waited; came

23 Different sounds

1 her; their, where • **2** hard; came, day • **3** shock; girl, hurt • **4** learn; weird, year • **5** kill; climb, drive • **6** land; art, far

24 Let's talk: Sich und andere beschreiben

► SB, p. 223

(*Lösungsbeispiel*) The person on the left is a girl with curly black hair. She looks quite tall. I think that she's good at maths and good with computers.
On the right I can see a boy with straight blond hair. He looks quite short. I think that he is good at drawing. I think that he is a very kind boy.

Unit 3: Activities and games

1 New words and phrases
▸ SB, pp. 78–79 | VOCABULARY pp. 251–252

1 beauty • 2 beast • 3 full of • 4 zip wire • 5 challenge • 6 took on the challenge • 7 a two-hour • 8 Insects • 9 book • 10 's on • 11 musical • 12 actor • 13 seat • 14 take a seat

2 What's the word?

1 three-week • 2 musical • 3 beautiful • 4 challenging • 5 sit

3 New words and phrases
▸ SB, p. 80 | VOCABULARY pp. 252–253

1 dungeons • 2 dragons • 3 role-play • 4 trains • 5 professional • 6 Castle • 7 knit • 8 course • 9 prepare for • 10 acting • 11 act • 12 photography • 13 sporty • 14 take place

4 New words and phrases
▸ SB, pp. 81–83 | VOCABULARY pp. 253–254

1 're going to; are; going to do • 2 camera • 3 tonight • 4 date • 5 somewhere

5 Bits and pieces

1 zip wire • 2 challenge • 3 role-play • 4 insect • 5 musical • 6 camera • 7 tonight • 8 dungeon

6 What's the right word?

1 full of • 2 two-hour • 3 seat • 4 somewhere • 5 beauty • 6 castle

7 New words and phrases
▸ SB, p. 84 | VOCABULARY p. 254

1 classical • 2 acoustic

8 New words and phrases
▸ SB, p. 85 | VOCABULARY p. 254

1 than • 2 the last one • 3 big one; small one • 4 green ones; red ones; yellow one • 5 lyrics • 6 energetic; energy • 7 worse • 8 better • 9 as good as • 10 Compare; with

9 Listen carefully!

1 challenging • 2 prepare • 3 photography • 4 camera • 5 musical • 6 actor • 7 professional • 8 castles • 9 date • 10 tonight

10 What's the word?

1 seat • 2 trainer • 3 booking • 4 prepare • 5 trains • 6 booked • 7 preparation • 8 sit

11 New words and phrases
▸ SB, p. 86 | VOCABULARY p. 254

1 science fiction / sci-fi • 2 rate • 3 ratings • 4 effect on • 5 special effects • 6 worst • 7 best • 8 space

12 New words and phrases
► SB, p. 87 | VOCABULARY p. 255

1 aliens • **2** magazines

13 What's the word: *one* or *ones*?

1 one; one; one; one • **2** ones; ones; ones • **3** ones

14 New words and phrases
► SB, p. 88 | VOCABULARY p. 255

1 real • **2** forest • **3** bridge • **4** stairs • **5** key • **6** keeps doing • **7** Turn right; turn left • **8** straight on • **9** past • **10** across

15 New words and phrases
► SB, p. 89 | VOCABULARY pp. 255–256

1 trophy • **2** trophies • **3** above • **4** above • **5** below • **6** bird • **7** square • **8** square • **9** score • **10** bottom • **11** level • **12** row

16 Opposites

1 bottom • **2** below • **3** worst • **4** better • **5** (to) be off • **6** unreal

17 Odd word out

1 tonight • **2** great • **3** dragon • **4** beauty • **5** character • **6** forest

18 New words and phrases
► SB, p. 90 | VOCABULARY pp. 256–257

1 until/till • **2** can't/cannot; until/till • **3** suggested; to her mother • **4** quarter to 7/seven • **5** quarter past 7/seven • **6** half past 6/six • **7** Match • **8** expert • **9** directions

19 Telling the time

1 quarter past 6/six • **2** 8/eight o'clock • **3** half past 3/three • **4** quarter to 10/ten • **5** half past 9/nine • **6** quarter to 7/seven • **7** 1/one o'clock • **8** quarter past 2/two • **9** quarter to 11/eleven

20 New words and phrases
► SB, p. 91 | VOCABULARY p. 257

1 international • **2** probably • **3** surf the web • **4** social media • **5** all over the world • **6** screen • **7** lingua franca • **8** situation

21 New words and phrases
► SB, p. 92 | VOCABULARY pp. 257–258

1 too much of a good thing • **2** chat with • **3** chatty • **4** bored • **5** cough • **6** have a headache • **7** Get better soon! / Get well soon! • **8** click on • **9** a while • **10** rules

22 New words and phrases
► SB, pp. 93–94 | VOCABULARY p. 258

1 What's wrong? • **2** calendar • **3** study • **4** come round • **5** puzzled • **6** marks • **7** ending • **8** don't use; any more

23 Lost words

1 in • **2** on; at • **3** on • **4** for; on • **5** out; in • **6** of • **7** in • **8** to • **9** on; to; on • **10** in • **11** at

24 What's the word?

1 marks • **2** click • **3** run • **4** challenge • **5** scored • **6** cough • **7** chats • **8** dating

25 New words and phrases

▶ SB, pp. 96–97 | VOCABULARY pp. 258–259

1 especially • **2** discuss • **3** should • **4** attention

26 Listen carefully!

1 straight • **2** square • **3** across; right • **4** bottom • **5** headache • **6** cough • **7** chat • **8** bored • **9** wrong • **10** puzzled

27 Let's talk: Sich verabreden: Vorschläge machen und darauf reagieren

▶ SB, p. 224

(*Lösungsbeispiel*)

Partner A: Hi. Can we meet today?
Partner B: Sorry, I can't. I'm really busy today.
Partner A: Are you doing anything special today?
Partner B: I'm helping my parents with the shopping.
Partner A: What are you doing this weekend?
Partner B: I'm not doing anything this weekend.
Partner A: Do you want to come round and have dinner with us this weekend?
Partner B: Oh yes, thanks for the invitation.
Partner A: Would Friday, Saturday or Sunday be best?
Partner B: Saturday would be best.
Partner A: Great. Bye. See you on Saturday.

28 Let's talk: Seine Meinung äußern und diskutieren

▶ SB, p. 226

1 I'm sorry, I don't agree.
2 What do you think?
3 That looks really/very interesting.
4 I agree with you.

1 New words and phrases
▶ SB, pp. 112–113 | VOCABULARY p. 259

1 celebrates • **2** celebration • **3** breaking; fast • **4** fast • **5** broke • **6** carnival • **7** Bonfires • **8** candles • **9** firework • **10** firework(s)

2 New words and phrases
▶ SB, p. 114 | VOCABULARY pp. 259–260

1 practising Muslims • **2** Are you thirsty? • **3** sunrise • **4** pray • **5** Thank • **6** charity • **7** flowers • **8** god

3 New words and phrases
▶ SB, p. 115 | VOCABULARY pp. 260–261

1 chocolate • **2** yoghurt • **3** each other • **4** pot • **5** jar • **6** juice • **7** biscuit • **8** bath • **9** carton • **10** baked beans • **11** mosque • **12** tin • **13** wish

4 New words and phrases
▶ SB, p. 116 | VOCABULARY p. 261

1 beef • **2** sheep • **3** lamb • **4** pork • **5** respect • **6** a few

5 New words and phrases
▶ SB, p. 117 | VOCABULARY p. 261

1 collection • **2** May I • **3** soups • **4** pancakes • **5** strange • **6** strangers

6 Bits and pieces

1 Muslim • **2** firework • **3** pancake • **4** sunrise • **5** carnival • **6** charity • **7** biscuit • **8** respect

7 New words and phrases
▶ SB, pp. 118–119 | VOCABULARY pp. 261–262

1 romantic • **2** surprise • **3** just • **4** So far • **5** finishes • **6** not; yet • **7** yet • **8** lose • **9** lost • **10** ’ve/have; lost • **11** blows • **12** blew • **13** has; blown

8 New words and phrases
▶ SB, pp. 120–121 | VOCABULARY p. 262

1 Poor • **2** feed • **3** fed • **4** Have; fed • **5** Both • **6** ever

9 What have they already done? What haven’t they done yet?
▶ SB, p. 266 (irregular verbs)

1 done; yet • **2** finished; started; yet • **3** eaten yet • **4** already fed • **5** taken; yet • **6** already blown up • **7** found; yet • **8** already given • **9** already bought • **10** been; yet; already made

10 Listen carefully!

1 celebrated • **2** celebration • **3** fireworks • **4** thirsty • **5** juice • **6** biscuits; chocolates • **7** beef; lamb • **8** soup; baked beans • **9** pancakes • **10** yoghurt

11 New words and phrases
▶ SB, pp. 122–123 | VOCABULARY pp. 262–263

1 cheesy • **2** member • **3** anybody/anyone • **4** anywhere • **5** nothing • **6** colourful • **7** hold • **8** Have; held • **9** held

12 Lost words

1 to • **2** during • **3** for • **4** in • **5** with • **6** up • **7** on • **8** onto • **9** from

13 What's the word: *any, anybody, anything* or *anywhere*?

1 anything • **2** any • **3** anywhere • **4** anybody

14 New words and phrases

► SB, p. 124 | VOCABULARY p. 263

1 christening • **2** house-warming (party) • **3** scare • **4** embarrassing

15 New words and phrases

► SB, p. 125 | VOCABULARY p. 263

1 bride • **2** bridegroom • **3** a suit • **4** niece; nephew • **5** bridesmaids • **6** groomsman • **7** groomsmen • **8** afterwards

16 New words and phrases

► SB, p. 126 | VOCABULARY pp. 263–264

1 on time • **2** put; on • **3** organizes • **4** awake • **5** for hours • **6** set the table • **7** looks at himself

17 New words and phrases

► SB, p. 127 | VOCABULARY pp. 264–265

1 Suddenly • **2** steal • **3** has stolen • **4** stole • **5** downstairs; upstairs • **6** Do; believe in • **7** lock • **8** pocket • **9** pocket money • **10** slippers • **11** as/when • **12** disappointed with • **13** for better or (for) worse • **14** sickness • **15** sick

18 Opposites

1 sunrise • **2** (to) lose • **3** downstairs • **4** (to) unlock • **5** awake • **6** (to) put sth. on • **7** never • **8** everything

19 New words and phrases

► SB, p. 128 | VOCABULARY p. 265

1 jacket • **2** multicultural • **3** scarf • **4** scarves • **5** global • **6** citizen

20 New words and phrases

► SB, pp. 130–131 | VOCABULARY p. 266

1 slides • **2** keywords • **3** ceremony • **4** order • **5** audio • **6** Visual

21 Listen carefully!

1 ceremony • **2** surprise • **3** collection • **4** multicultural • **5** organizing • **6** wife; citizen • **7** Muslims • **8** mosque • **9** Suddenly • **10** romantic

22 Let's talk: Beim Essen und bei Tisch

► SB, p. 225

(*Lösungsbeispiel*)

1. Could I have some orange juice, please?
2. May I have some salad, please?
3. Would you like some potatoes?
4. Yes, please.
5. Enjoy your meal!

23 Let's talk: Feedback geben

► SB, p. 227

(*Lösungsbeispiel*)

1 You've done a great job!
2 I understood everything that you said.
3 You looked at the audience.
4 You spoke loudly and clearly.
5 You smiled.
6 The text on your slides was a bit small.

Unit 5: Getting ready for the future

1 New words and phrases

► SB, pp. 144–145 | VOCABULARY pp. 266–267

1 future • **2** builder • **3** firefighter • **4** hairdresser • **5** mechanic

2 New words and phrases

► SB, pp. 146–149 | VOCABULARY pp. 267–268

1 I want to be a nurse. • **2** police officer • **3** architect • **4** I'll be / I will be • **5** won't / will not • **6** manager • **7** crazy • **8** predictions • **9** earns • **10** imagine • **11** successful • **12** come true

3 New words and phrases

► SB, pp. 150–152 | VOCABULARY pp. 268–269

1 conversation • **2** explanation • **3** chores • **4** Fold • **5** wash • **6** does the washing • **7** babysit • **8** babysitting • **9** empty; dishwasher • **10** empty • **11** vacuum • **12** vacuum cleaner • **13** have to • **14** bar chart • **15** horizontal • **16** axes; axis; axis • **17** vertical • **18** large • **19** I don't mind

4 Listen carefully!

1 predictions • **2** future • **3** nurse • **4** earn • **5** mind • **6** imagine • **7** successful • **8** come true • **9** chores • **10** dishwasher

5 New words and phrases

► SB, p. 153 | VOCABULARY p. 269

1 typical • **2** typical of • **3** corner shop • **4** That's when • **5** sell • **6** have sold/sold • **7** have sold • **8** early • **9** shop assistant; size

6 New words and phrases

► SB, p. 154 | VOCABULARY pp. 269–270

1 treat • **2** treat • **3** shop • **4** per cent • **5** spotlights • **6** in/under the spotlight • **7** pay (in) cash • **8** cash machine • **9** walk the dog • **10** mustn't • **11** savings account • **12** coins • **13** piggy bank

7 What are the words: *That's when – That's why – That's what – That's how?*

1 That's why • **2** That's how • **3** that's what • **4** That's when

8 What are the words: *must, mustn't* or *don't have to?*

1 don't have to • **2** must • **3** mustn't • **4** don't have to • **5** mustn't

9 New words and phrases

► SB, p. 155 | VOCABULARY pp. 270–271

1 paint • **2** paint • **3** bakery • **4** Bakers • **5** electronics • **6** gift/present • **7** gift shop • **8** newsagent • **9** newsagent's • **10** comfortable

10 Word search

1 vacuums • **2** earn • **3** built • **4** empty • **5** baking • **6** have; folded • **7** sold • **8** Wash

11 New words and phrases

► SB, p. 156 | VOCABULARY pp. 271–272

1 How much is • **2** How much are • **3** brand • **4** Could you • **5** try on • **6** changing room • **7** change • **8** receipt

12 Lost words

1 for • **2** on • **3** about • **4** about • **5** at • **6** of • **7** to • **8** in; by • **9** of • **10** to; of

13 Different sounds

1 clear; hurt, learn • **2** know; moon, new • **3** hour; door, false • **4** bread; bean, three • **5** five; fifth, trip

14 New words and phrases

► SB, p. 157 | VOCABULARY p. 272

1 price • **2** postcard • **3** shorts • **4** customer

15 New words and phrases

► SB, pp. 158–159 | VOCABULARY pp. 272–273

1 has gone • **2** 's/is gone • **3** miss • **4** missed • **5** move to • **6** such a • **7** Follow • **8** annoy • **9** independent of • **10** bowl • **11** business

16 New words and phrases

► SB, p. 160 | VOCABULARY p. 273

1 connection • **2** connect; to • **3** repeat • **4** strength • **5** strong • **6** solve • **7** solution

17 Listen carefully!

1 sold • **2** comfortable • **3** savings account • **4** independent • **5** bakery • **6** cash machine • **7** per cent • **8** business • **9** repeat • **10** strengths

18 New words and phrases

► SB, pp. 162–163 | VOCABULARY pp. 273–274

1 looks forward to • **2** look forward to hearing • **3** luckily • **4** horoscopes • **5** star sign • **6** pronunciation • **7** pronounce • **8** dictionary • **9** imaginative • **10** curious about • **11** tolerant of • **12** dramatic • **13** practical • **14** sociable • **15** generous

19 Picture crossword

1 coin • **2** shorts • **3** cash machine • **4** dishwasher • **5** hairdresser • **6** driver • **7** piggy bank • **8** dancer • **9** spotlight • **10** newsagent's • **11** mechanic • **12** bowl • **13** architect • **14** bakery • **15** photographer • **16** nurse

20 What are the words?

1 (to) buy sth. • **2** a conversation / a chat • **3** (to) walk the dog • **4** a gift • **5** (to) repeat sth. • **6** a bakery • **7** changing room • **8** (to) annoy sb. • **9** dishwasher • **10** newsagent's

21 What did they do yesterday evening?

1 went; babysat • **2** spent; made; ate; felt; came • **3** had; sang • **4** was; read; told

22 Opposites

1 independent • **2** uncomfortable • **3** intolerant • **4** (to) sell • **5** (to) pay by card • **6** early

23 Let's talk: Über Berufe und die Zukunft sprechen

► SB, p. 226

(*Lösungsbeispiel*)

When I was little, I wanted to be a teacher / a firefighter / a … . Now I want to be a computer programmer / a nurse / a … . My mum is a shop assistant / a designer / a singer / a … . My dad is a builder / a driver / a dancer / a … . In the future I'll have a wife/husband and two children. Maybe I'll have a house in the country.

24 Let's talk: Einkaufen und über Preise sprechen

► SB, p. 227

(*Lösungsbeispiel*)

Bild 1:

A: Can I **help you**?
B: Yes, please. Do you **have these trousers in size M**?
A: I'll go and see if we have them in size M. What about the dress?
B: Do you have **it in blue**?
A: Here you are.
B: Thank you. Can I **try them on**?
A: Yes, of course, the **changing rooms** are over there.

Bild 2:

C: How would you like to pay?
B: I'd like **to pay by card**.
C: OK. Put your card here, please.
B: I'd **like a receipt**, please.
C: No problem.
B: Can I have a **bag, please**?
C: Sure.
B: **Thank you. Goodbye**.
C: Bye.

°Unit 6: The treasure hunt

1 New words and phrases

► SB, pp. 176–177 | VOCABULARY pp. 274–275

1 treasure hunt • **2** Nature reserves • **3** pretty • **4** Shout • **5** trails • **6** divided; into • **7** hid • **8** clues • **9** along the trail • **10** handed; out to us • **11** Good luck • **12** counting-out rhymes • **13** hers • **14** chanted • **15** ducks • **16** decided to • **17** without

2 Scrambled words

1 Nature Reserve • **2** pretty • **3** hidden treasure; tourists

3 New words and phrases

► SB, p. 178 | VOCABULARY pp. 275–276

1 pointed to/at • **2** pond • **3** leads • **4** led • **5** bush • **6** bell • **7** grass • **8** Look up

4 New words and phrases

► SB, pp. 179–180 | VOCABULARY p. 276

1 dandelion(s) • **2** bench • **3** catch • **4** caught • **5** factory

5 New words and phrases

► SB, p. 181 | VOCABULARY p. 276

1 Congratulations on • **2** results • **3** clapped (their hands) • **4** We did it! • **5** teammates • **6** cheat

6 Listen carefully!

1 treasure hunt • **2** have hidden • **3** hid; along the trail • **4** divided; into • **5** led; led • **6** leader; without • **7** pond; bush • **8** grass; dandelions • **9** teammates; bench • **10** clapped; Congratulations

7 Lost words

1 up • **2** into • **3** in • **4** along • **5** out • **6** At • **7** of • **8** at • **9** to

15 New words and phrases

► SB, p. 89 | VOCABULARY pp. 255–256

1	"Is this your ____________, Max?" – "No, it isn't."	„Ist das dein **Pokal**, Max?" – „Nein."
2	Sina is a very good tennis player. She has lots of ____________.	Sina ist eine sehr gute Tennisspielerin. Sie besitzt viele **Pokale**.
3	We live on the top floor. There is nobody ____________ us.	Wir wohnen im obersten Stockwerk. **Über** uns ist niemand.
4	Read the instructions ____________.	Lies die Anweisungen **oben**.
5	Find a title for the text ____________.	Finde eine Überschrift für den Text **unten**.
6	A seagull is a big ____________ that lives by the sea.	Eine Möwe ist ein großer **Vogel**, der am Meer lebt.
7	Our kitchen is a ____________ room.	Unsere Küche ist ein **rechteckiger** Raum.
8	Can we meet in the market ____________?	Können wir uns am Markt**platz** treffen?
9	What's the ____________?	Wie ist der **Punktestand**?
10	The station is at the ____________ of the street.	Der Bahnhof ist am **unteren Ende** der Straße.
11	Tom is proud when he gets to the next ____________ in his computer game.	Tom ist stolz, wenn er das nächste **Level** in seinem Computerspiel erreicht.
12	I never sit in the last ____________ on a bus.	Ich sitze nie in der letzten **Reihe** im Bus.

16 Opposites

Finde die Gegenteile.

1 top ◄► ____________
2 above ◄► ____________
3 best ◄► ____________
4 worse ◄► ____________
5 (to) be on ◄► ____________
6 real ◄► ____________

17 Odd word out

Unterstreiche das Wort, das nicht in die Reihe passt.

1 yesterday – tonight – today – tomorrow
2 terrible – horrible – bad – great
3 goat – cat – dragon – horse
4 creative – energetic – musical – beauty
5 doctor – character – teacher – actor
6 theatre – audience – forest – actor

18 New words and phrases

► SB, p. 90 | VOCABULARY pp. 256–257

1	You can watch TV ______________ I come home.	Du kannst fernsehen, **bis** ich nach Hause komme.
2	We ______________ play outside ______________ the rain stops.	Wir **können erst** draußen spielen, **wenn** der Regen aufhört.
3	Liz ______________ meeting online ______________.	Liz **schlug ihrer Mutter vor**, sich online zu treffen.
4	On weekdays I get up at ______________.	An Wochentagen stehe ich um **viertel vor 7** auf.
5	I leave the house at ______________.	Ich verlasse das Haus um **viertel nach 7**.
6	On weekdays I come home at ______________.	Wochentags komme ich um **halb 7** nach Hause.
7	______________ the words to the pictures.	**Ordne** die Wörter den Bildern **zu**.
8	Sina is a computer ______________.	Sina ist Computer**expertin**.
9	Can you send me a message with ______________ to your house?	Kannst du mir eine Nachricht mit einer **Wegbeschreibung** zu deinem Haus schicken?

19 Telling the time

Wie lautet jeweils die Uhrzeit auf Englisch? Schreibe sie unter die Zifferblätter.

1

____

2

____

3

____

4

____

5

____

6

____

7

____

8

____

9

____

► Check

20 New words and phrases

► SB, p. 91 | VOCABULARY p. 257

1	Frankfurt has an ____________ airport.	Frankfurt hat einen **internationalen** Flughafen.
2	You ____________ know that you can't bring your cat to school.	Du weißt **wahrscheinlich**, dass du deine Katze nicht in die Schule mitbringen kannst.
3	How often do you ____________?	Wie oft **surfst du im Internet**?
4	What do you do on ____________?	Was machst du **in den sozialen Medien**?
5	Farid has friends ____________.	Farid hat Freunde **auf der ganzen Welt**.
6	I don't watch films on my phone because the ____________ is too small.	Ich schaue keine Filme auf meinem Handy, weil der **Bildschirm** zu klein ist.
7	Lots of people use English as a ____________ ____________.	Viele Menschen verwenden Englisch als **Lingua Franca**.
8	Ben stays calm in any ____________.	Ben bleibt in jeder **Situation** ruhig.

21 New words and phrases

► SB, p. 92 | VOCABULARY pp. 257–258

1	Eating ice cream every day is ____________ ____________.	Jeden Tag Eis essen ist **zu viel des Guten**.
2	I often ____________ my best friend in the evening.	Ich **chatte** abends oft **mit** meiner besten Freundin.
3	Our neighbour is quite ____________.	Unser Nachbar ist ziemlich **geschwätzig**.
4	I was so ____________ by the talk that I nearly fell asleep.	Ich war so **gelangweilt** von dem Vortrag, dass ich fast eingeschlafen wäre.
5	The baby has a bad ____________.	Das Baby hat einen schlimmen **Husten**.
6	I can't do sport today because I ____________ ____________.	Ich kann heute keinen Sport machen, da ich **Kopfschmerzen habe**.
7	____________!	**Gute Besserung!**
8	If you need more information, ____________ ____________ the link.	Wenn Sie weitere Informationen benötigen, **klicken** Sie **auf** den Link.
9	We lived in London for ____________.	Wir haben **eine Weile** in London gelebt.
10	I don't know the ____________ of rugby.	Ich kenne die Rugby-**Regeln** nicht.

22 New words and phrases

▸ SB, pp. 93–94 | VOCABULARY p. 258

1	You look sad. ______________________?	Du siehst traurig aus. **Was ist los?**
2	"Are you free on Tuesday?" – "Let me check my _______________."	„Hast du am Dienstag Zeit?" – „Lass mich meinen **Kalender** checken."
3	Tom wants to _______________ art.	Tom möchte Kunst **studieren**.
4	Can I _______________ this afternoon?	Kann ich heute Nachmittag **vorbeikommen**?
5	Mara was _______________ when she didn't get an invitation to Tom's party.	Mara war **verwundert**, als sie keine Einladung zu Toms Party bekam.
6	Tarek is a hard-working student. He always gets good _______________.	Tarek ist ein fleißiger Schüler. Er bekommt immer gute **Noten**.
7	I like the book because it has a happy _______________.	Ich mag das Buch, weil es ein glückliches **Ende** hat.
8	This phone is very old. I _______________ it _______________.	Das Handy ist sehr alt. Ich **benutze** es **nicht mehr**.

23 Lost words

Vervollständige die Sätze mit den Wörtern aus den Luftballons.

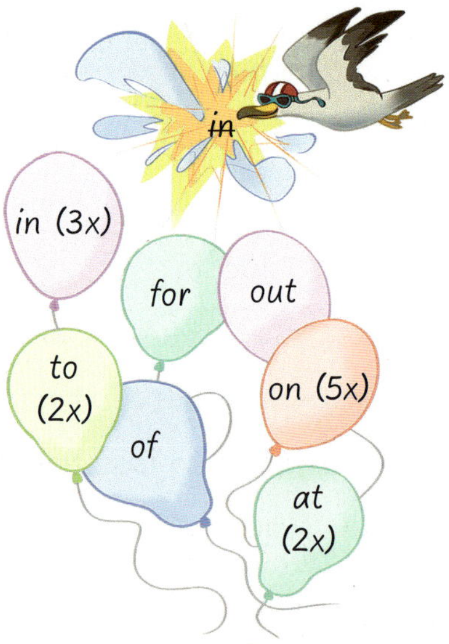

1 We booked a holiday flat ___*in*___ Brighton.
2 What's __________ at the cinema __________ the moment?
3 Doing sports always has a good effect __________ me.
4 I want to prepare __________ the English test __________ Monday.
5 We often act __________ dialogues __________ front of the class.
6 The theatre was full __________ young people.
7 The next show takes place __________ March.
8 I went __________ Italy last summer.
9 Match the texts __________ the left __________ the pictures __________ the right.
10 Tom would like to act __________ the school play.
11 Lara is very good __________ maths.

▸ Check

24 What's the word?

challenge • chat • click • cough • date • mark • run • score

Vervollständige die Sätze mit den Wörtern aus dem Kasten. Achte auf die Form.

1 Sam is a hard-working student. His teachers give him good ______________.
2 Think hard before you ______________ on a link!
3 Sarah goes for a ______________ every morning to keep fit.
4 Travelling alone can be quite a ______________ for a ten-year-old child.
5 Tim won the game last night. He ______________ 10 points.
6 Rula has a ______________ and a headache and can't go to school today.
7 Tarek often ______________ with his friends on Sunday afternoons.
8 Is Peter ______________ Melissa?

25 New words and phrases

▸ SB, pp. 96–97 | VOCABULARY pp. 258–259

1	I love animals, ______________ elephants.	Ich liebe Tiere, **besonders** Elefanten.
2	Let's ______________ the problem in class.	Lasst uns das Problem im Unterricht **besprechen**.
3	You ______________ take singing lessons.	Du **solltest** Gesangsunterricht nehmen.
4	Hello everybody! Can I have your ______________, please?	Hallo zusammen! Kann ich bitte eure **Aufmerksamkeit** haben?

26 Listen carefully!

07

Höre dir die Sätze aufmerksam an und schreibe das fehlende Wort in die Lücke.

1 Turn left at the cinema and then go ______________ on.
2 Keep going until you come to a big ______________.
3 Walk ______________ it and turn ______________ into Theatre Street.
4 Our house is at the ______________ of the street.
5 Sally can't go to school today because she has a ______________.
6 Sally's brother has a bad ______________.
7 Sarah can't ______________ with her friends today.
8 She is ______________.
9 Sarah's friends don't know what's ______________ with her.
10 They're ______________.

27 Let's talk: Sich verabreden: Vorschläge machen und darauf reagieren

► SB, p. 224

Partner A möchte sich mit Partner B verabreden. Schreibe ihren Dialog mit den Sätzen aus dem Kasten in dein Heft. Du kannst deinen Dialog auch aufnehmen und jemanden bitten, ihn sich anzuhören und dir Feedback zu geben.

I'm helping my parents with the shopping. • Saturday would be best. • Oh yes, thanks for the invitation. • Do you want to come round and have dinner with us this weekend? • Great. Bye. See you on Saturday. • I'm not doing anything this weekend. • Sorry, I can't. • Would Friday, Saturday or Sunday be best? • Are you doing anything special today? • ~~Hi! Can we meet today?~~ • I'm really busy today. • What are you doing this weekend?

28 Let's talk: Seine Meinung äußern und diskutieren

► SB, p. 226

Sieh dir die Fragen unten an und beantworte sie. Du kannst deine Antworten auch aufnehmen und jemanden bitten, sie sich anzuhören und dir Feedback zu geben.

Was sagst du auf Englisch, wenn ...

1 ... du sagen möchtest, dass du anderer Meinung bist?

____

2 ... du fragen möchtest, was dein/e Gesprächspartner/in über eine Sache denkt?

____

3 ... du sagen möchtest, dass etwas sehr interessant aussieht?

____

4 ... du sagen möchtest, dass du deinem/deiner Gesprächspartner/in zustimmst?

____

► Check

Unit 4
Celebrate!

1 New words and phrases

▸ SB, pp. 112–113 | VOCABULARY p. 259

1	Tom ____________ his birthday every year.	Tom **feiert** jedes Jahr seinen Geburtstag.
2	Tom spends a lot of time preparing his ____________.	Tom verbringt viel Zeit damit, seine **Feier** vorzubereiten.
3	We enjoy ____________ the ____________ with all the family.	Wir genießen das **Fastenbrechen** mit der ganzen Familie.
4	Jamal started to ____________ when he was 14 years old.	Jamal begann zu **fasten**, als er 14 Jahre alt war.
5	The wind was so strong last night that my bedroom window ____________.	Der Wind war so stark letzte Nacht, dass mein Schlafzimmerfenster **zerbrochen ist**.
6	Zola makes her own ____________ costumes.	Zola macht ihre **Karnevals**kostüme selbst.
7	____________ can be dangerous for animals.	**Freudenfeuer** können gefährlich für Tiere sein.
8	We put real ____________ on our Christmas tree.	Wir machen echte **Kerzen** an unseren Weihnachtsbaum.
9	Don't touch this ____________!	Fass den **Feuerwerkskörper** nicht an!
10	There is a ____________ competition in our town every summer.	In unserer Stadt gibt es jeden Sommer einen **Feuerwerks**wettbewerb.

2 New words and phrases

▸ SB, p. 114 | VOCABULARY pp. 259–260

1	Farid and Mariam are ____________ ____________.	Farid und Mariam sind **praktizierende Muslime**.
2	____________?	**Hast du Durst?**
3	I never get up before ____________.	Ich stehe nie vor **Sonnenaufgang** auf.
4	Let's ____________ for this war to stop.	Lasst uns dafür **beten**, dass dieser Krieg endet.
5	____________ Grandma for the present.	**Bedanke** dich bei Oma für das Geschenk.
6	Cem works for a ____________.	Cem arbeitet für eine **wohltätige Organisation**.
7	We have lots of ____________ in our garden.	Wir haben viele **Blumen** in unserem Garten.
8	Neptun is the ____________ of the sea.	Neptun ist der **Gott** des Meeres.

3 New words and phrases

▸ SB, p. 115 | VOCABULARY pp. 260–261

Lies die Sätze, sieh dir die Bilder an und trage die richtigen Wörter in das Gitter ein.

1

2

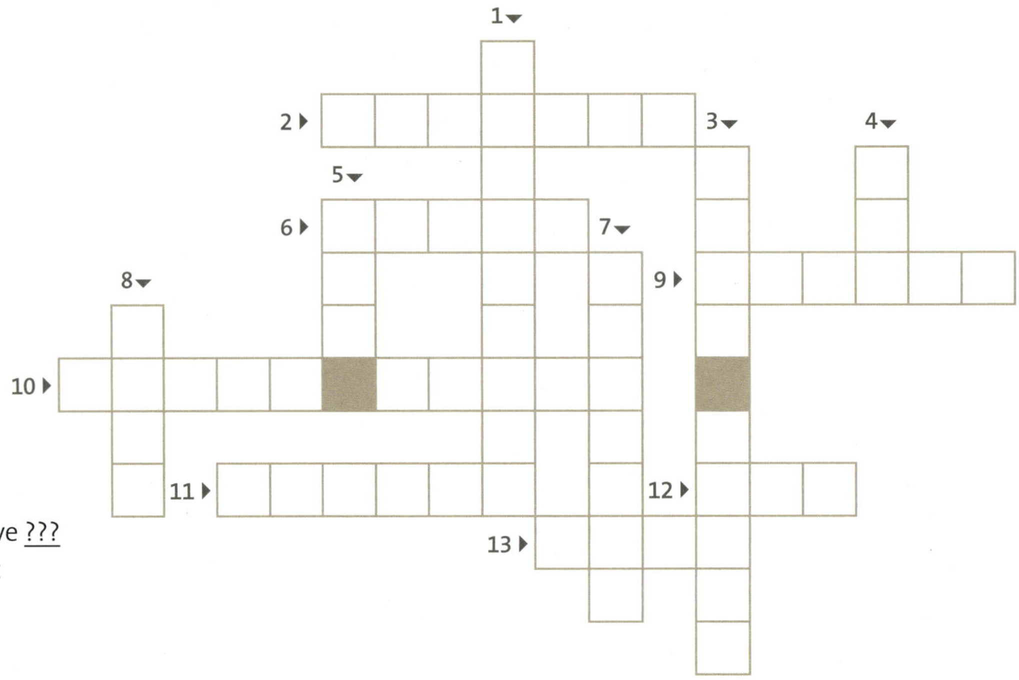

3 Dan and Mia love ??? and want to get married soon.

4

5

6

7

8

9

10

11

12

13 I ??? you a happy birthay!

▸ Check

4 New words and phrases

▸ SB, p. 116 | VOCABULARY p. 261

Schreibe auf, was gemeint ist.

1 meat from cows: ______________________

2 a farm animal that gives us cheese, meat and wool[1]: ______________________

3 a young one of number **2**: ______________________

4 meat from pigs: ______________________

5 thinking well of someone: having ______________________ for someone

6 another way to say "some, but not many": ______________________

[1] **wool** *Wolle*

5 New words and phrases

▸ SB, p. 117 | VOCABULARY p. 261

1	Ron has a big elephant ______________________.	Ron hat eine große Elefanten-**Sammlung**.
2	______________________ watch TV tonight?	**Darf ich** heute Abend fernsehen?
3	Grandpa makes great ______________________.	Opa kocht tolle **Suppen**.
4	I love Grandma's ______________________.	Ich liebe Omas **Pfannkuchen**.
5	Do you hear that ______________________ noise?	Hörst du das **seltsame** Geräusch?
6	Our neighbours came as ______________________, but soon became good friends.	Unsere Nachbarn kamen als **Fremde**, wurden aber bald gute Freunde.

6 Bits and pieces

Verbinde die Teile miteinander, um Wörter zu bilden.

Mus – fire – pan – sun – carni – char – bis – re

val – spect – lim – cuit – cake – work – rise – ity

7 New words and phrases

▶ SB, pp. 118–119 | VOCABULARY pp. 261–262

1 Yara and Joe's wedding was very ____________________.	Yaras und Joes Hochzeit war sehr **romantisch**.
2 Yara's parents had a big ____________________ for Yara and Joe: a trip to Venice.	Yaras Eltern hatten eine große **Überraschung** für Yara und Joe: eine Reise nach Venedig.
3 I've ____________________ started to do my homework.	Ich habe **gerade** begonnen, meine Hausaufgaben zu machen.
4 __________________ everything has been easy.	**Bis jetzt** war alles einfach.
5 The concert __________________ at 10 p.m.	Das Konzert **endet** um 22 Uhr.
6 The lesson has __________________ started __________________.	Die Unterrichtsstunde hat **noch nicht** begonnen.
7 Have you done your homework ____________?	Hast du **schon** deine Hausaufgaben gemacht?
8 Our team is great. We never ________________ a single game.	Unser Team ist großartig. Wir **verlieren** kein einziges Spiel.
9 Jamie's team was sad when it ____________________ the match.	Jamies Team war traurig, als es das Spiel **verlor**.
10 I _____________ just _____________ my key.	Ich **habe** gerade meinen Schlüssel **verloren**.
11 It's noisy here when the wind ______________.	Es ist laut hier, wenn der Wind **weht**.
12 A strong wind __________________ all week.	Die ganze Woche **wehte** ein starker Wind.
13 The wind ____________________ just ____________________ away my hat.	Der Wind **hat** gerade meinen Hut weg**geblasen**.

8 New words and phrases

▶ SB, pp. 120–121 | VOCABULARY p. 262

1 __________________ Molly has broken her leg.	Die **arme** Molly hat sich das Bein gebrochen.
2 I ________________ the cat before I go to work.	Ich **füttere** die Katze, bevor ich zur Arbeit gehe.
3 When our neighbours were on holiday, we __________________ their animals.	Als unsere Nachbarn im Urlaub waren, **fütterten** wir ihre Tiere.
4 ______________ you _____________ the dog?	**Hast** du den Hund **gefüttert**?
5 ______________ my sisters are doctors.	Meine **beiden** Schwestern sind Ärztinnen.
6 Have you _________________ swum in a river?	Bist du **jemals** in einem Fluss geschwommen?

▶ Check

9 What have they already done? What haven't they done yet?

▸ SB, p. 266 (irregular verbs)

Vervollständige die Aussagesätze und Fragen mit dem *past participle* des Verbs in Klammern und *already* oder *yet*.

1 Have you ______________ (do) your homework ______________?

2 I've ______________ (finish) maths, but I haven't ______________ (start) my art presentation ______________.

3 Have you ______________ (eat) ______________?

4 Don't feed the dog. I've ______________ ______________ (feed) him.

5 Have you ______________ (take) him for a walk ______________?

6 Do we really need more ballons? I've ______________ ______________ (blow up) twenty-five red ones and twenty blue ones.

7 Have you ______________ (find) your phone ______________?

8 No, but my sister has ______________ ______________ (give) me her old one.

9 It's Lisa's birthday next week. I've ______________ ______________ (buy) a nice present for her.

10 I haven't ______________ (be) into town ______________ to buy something for her, but I've ______________ ______________ (make) a card for her.

10 Listen carefully!

08

Höre dir die Sätze aufmerksam an und schreibe das fehlende Wort in die Lücke.

1 Grandpa ______________ his 80th birthday last Saturday.

2 It was a very special ______________.

3 We even had ______________ in the evening.

4 It was a hot day, so everybody was very ______________.

5 We drank lots of orange and apple ______________.

6 In the afternoon we had ______________ and ______________.

7 In the evening we ate ______________ and ______________ with potatoes and vegetables.

8 There was ______________, salad and ______________ for people who didn't want to eat meat.

9 For dessert we had ______________ with ice cream.

10 There was also ______________ with fruit.

11 New words and phrases

▸ SB, pp. 122–123 | VOCABULARY pp. 262–263

1	Moira likes __________ love songs.	Moira mag **kitschige** Liebeslieder.
2	Lara is a __________ of a tennis club.	Lara ist **Mitglied** in einem Tennisverein.
3	Has __________ called for me?	Hat **jemand** für mich angerufen?
4	I can't go __________ before I have finished my homework.	Ich kann **nirgendwo** hingehen, bevor ich nicht meine Hausaufgaben gemacht habe.
5	There is __________ in my bag.	In meiner Tasche ist **nichts**.
6	Rishi likes __________ shirts.	Rishi mag **bunte** Hemden.
7	May I __________ the baby?	Darf ich das Baby **halten**?
8	__________ you ever __________ a baby?	**Hast** du schon einmal ein Baby **gehalten**?
9	Zoe __________ my hand when we got on the train.	Zoe **hielt** meine Hand, als wir in den Zug einstiegen.

12 Lost words

Vervollständige die Sätze mit den Wörtern aus den Luftballons.

1 Moira has invited me _to_ her birthday party.
2 Don't look at your phone __________ the concert.
3 Show respect __________ the musicians and the audience.
4 A lot of people have been ill __________ the last few weeks.
5 Sina surprised her friends __________ a cake.
6 Could you blow __________ a few balloons, please?
7 Doing sport has a positive effect __________ your health.
8 I never let my cat jump __________ the kitchen table.
9 Children learn a lot __________ each other.

13 What's the word: *any, anybody, anything* or *anywhere*?

Vervollständige die Sätze mit den richtigen Wörtern.

1 Would you like __________ else? – No thanks, I'm fine.
2 Do you have __________ questions?
3 Have you seen my bag? I can't find it __________.
4 I was a bit unhappy at the party because I didn't know __________.

▸ Check

14 New words and phrases

▸ SB, p. 124 | VOCABULARY p. 263

1	Sina went to her cousin's ______________.	Sina war auf der **Taufe** ihrer Cousine.
2	Our new neighbours have invited us to their ______________.	Unsere neuen Nachbarn haben uns zu ihrer **Einzugsfeier** eingeladen.
3	It's not funny to ______________ your sister. Stop it.	Es ist nicht lustig, deine Schwester zu **erschrecken**. Hör auf damit.
4	Some kids find their parents ______________.	Manche Kinder finden ihre Eltern **peinlich**.

15 New words and phrases

▸ SB, p. 125 | VOCABULARY p. 263

1	The ______________ wore a long white dress.	Die **Braut** trug ein langes weißes Kleid.
2	The ______________ was very excited.	Der **Bräutigam** war sehr aufgeregt.
3	Do you wear ______________ to work?	Trägst du **einen Anzug** zur Arbeit?
4	Your brother's or sister's daughter is your ______________, their son is your ______________.	Die Tochter deines Bruders oder deiner Schwester ist deine **Nichte**, ihr Sohn ist dein **Neffe**.
5	The ______________ wore green dresses.	Die **Brautjungfern** trugen grüne Kleider.
6	Ian asked his brother to be his ______________.	Ian bat seinen Bruder, sein **Trauzeuge** zu sein.
7	The ______________ prepared some games for the wedding party.	Die **Trauzeugen** bereiteten ein paar Spiele für die Hochzeitsfeier vor.
8	Let's do our homework now and go climbing ______________.	Lass uns jetzt unsere Hausaufgaben machen und **danach** klettern gehen.

16 New words and phrases

▸ SB, p. 126 | VOCABULARY pp. 263–264

1	The concert started ______________.	Das Konzert begann **pünktlich**.
2	Please ______________ your shoes ______________.	Bitte **ziehe** deine Schuhe **an**.
3	Jill ______________ lots of weddings.	Jill **organisiert** viele Hochzeiten.
4	Tom was still ______________ when Liz came home.	Tom war noch **wach**, als Liz heimkam.
5	Why have you been on the phone ______________?	Wieso hast du **stundenlang** telefoniert?
6	Please ______________.	Bitte **decke den Tisch**.
7	Jim often ______________ in the mirror.	Jim **sieht sich** oft im Spiegel **an**.

17 New words and phrases

► SB, p. 127 | VOCABULARY pp. 264–265

1	______________ I felt very tired.	**Plötzlich** war ich sehr müde.
2	Don't ______________ other people's ideas.	**Stiehl** nicht anderer Leute Ideen.
3	Sarah is angry because someone ______________ ______________ her bike.	Sarah ist wütend, weil jemand ihr Fahrrad **gestohlen hat**.
4	Kim ______________ a book.	Kim **stahl** ein Buch.
5	Our living room and kitchen are ______________, bedrooms and bathroom are ______________.	Unser Wohnzimmer und unsere Küche sind **unten**, Schlafzimmer und Bad sind **oben**.
6	______________ you ______________ god?	**Glaubst** du **an** Gott?
7	Please ______________ the door when you leave the house.	Bitte **schließe** die Tür **ab**, wenn du das Haus verlässt.
8	My school blazer only has one ______________.	Mein Schulblazer hat nur eine **Tasche**.
9	Do you get ______________________________?	Bekommst du **Taschengeld**?
10	Put your ______________ on, please.	Zieh bitte deine **Hausschuhe** an.
11	The girls laughed ______________ they danced.	Die Mädchen lachten, **während** sie tanzten.
12	Sarah was ______________________ her present.	Sarah war **enttäuscht von** ihrem Geschenk.
13	Your parents will always be there for you, ______________________________.	Deine Eltern werden immer für dich da sein, **was auch immer geschieht**.
14	Travel ______________ is something horrible.	Reise**krankheit** ist etwas Schreckliches.
15	A ______________ child can't go to school.	Ein **krankes** Kind kann nicht zur Schule gehen.

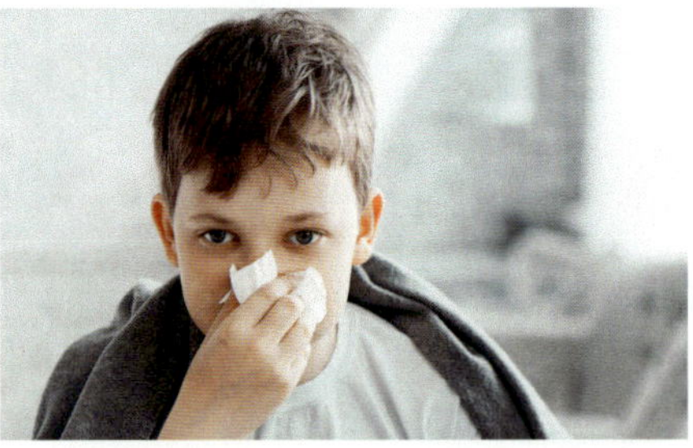

18 Opposites

Finde die Gegenteile.

1 sunset ◄► ______________

2 (to) win ◄► ______________

3 upstairs ◄► ______________

4 (to) lock ◄► ______________

5 asleep ◄► ______________

6 (to) take sth. off ◄► ______________

7 ever ◄► ______________

8 nothing ◄► ______________

► Check

19 New words and phrases

▸ SB, p. 128 | VOCABULARY p. 265

1	It's cold outside. You need a ______________.	Es ist kalt draußen. Du brauchst eine **Jacke**.
2	Joe lives in a ______________ neighbourhood.	Joe wohnt in einem **multikulturellen** Stadtteil.
3	I always wear a ______________ in winter.	Im Winter trage ich immer einen **Schal**.
4	I have lots of different ______________.	Ich habe viele verschiedene **Schals**.
5	Hunger is a ______________ problem.	Hunger ist ein **weltweites** Problem.
6	Tarek is a British ______________.	Tarek ist britischer **Staatsbürger**.

20 New words and phrases

▸ SB, pp. 130–131 | VOCABULARY p. 266

1	Don't use more than five ______________ for a ten-minute presentation.	Verwende nicht mehr als fünf **Folien** für eine zehnminütige Präsentation.
2	Use ______________ for your talk.	Verwende **Stichwörter** für deinen Vortrag.
3	Everybody enjoyed the wedding ______________.	Alle genossen die Hochzeits**feier**.
4	Put the words in the right ______________.	Bringe die Wörter in die richtige **Reihenfolge**.
5	I like listening to ______________ clips.	Ich höre mir gern **Audio**clips an.
6	______________ effects make your talk more interesting.	**Visuelle** Effekte machen deinen Vortrag interessanter.

09

21 Listen carefully!

Höre dir die Sätze aufmerksam an und schreibe das fehlende Wort in die Lücke.

1. My friend has invited me to his wedding ______________.
2. I want to buy him a ______________ present.
3. Maybe I can buy him something for his modern art ______________.
4. My friend comes from a ______________ family.
5. His brothers and sisters are ______________ a big party.
6. His ______________ isn't a British ______________ yet.
7. Both my friend and his partner are ______________.
8. I've never been in a ______________.
9. ______________ lots of my friends are getting married.
10. I love ______________ events.

▸ Check

22 Let's talk: Beim Essen und bei Tisch

► SB, p. 225

Sieh dir das Bild an und schreibe passende Fragen und Antworten in die Sprechblasen.

23 Let's talk: Feedback geben

► SB, p. 227

**Ein/e Klassenkamerad/in hat eine Präsentation auf Englisch gehalten.
Welches Feedback kannst du ihm/ihr im Anschluss daran auf Englisch geben?
Schreibe es auf die jeweilige Zeile.**

1 Das hast du toll gemacht: ____________________

2 Ich habe alles verstanden, was du gesagt hast: ____________________

____

3 Du hast das Publikum angesehen: ____________________

4 Du hast laut und deutlich gesprochen: ____________________

5 Du hast gelächelt: ____________________

6 Der Text auf deinen Folien war etwas zu klein: ____________________

____

► Check

Unit 5
Getting ready for the future

1 New words and phrases

► SB, pp. 144–145 | VOCABULARY pp. 266–267

1 Let's work together in the ____________.	Lass uns in **Zukunft** zusammenarbeiten.
2 Joe's father is a ____________________.	Joes Vater ist **Bauarbeiter**.
3 Joe is a ____________________.	Joe ist **Feuerwehrmann**.
4 Joe's brother is a ____________________.	Joes Bruder ist **Friseur**.
5 Joe's wife is a car ____________________.	Joes Frau ist Auto**mechanikerin**.

2 New words and phrases

► SB, pp. 146–149 | VOCABULARY pp. 267–268

1 ____________________________________.	**Ich möchte Krankenschwester/Krankenpfleger werden.**
2 You should be sporty if you want to be a ____________________________________.	Du solltest sportlich sein, wenn du **Polizeibeamter/Polizeibeamtin** werden möchtest.
3 As an ____________________ you need to be good at maths and drawing.	Als **Architekt/in** musst du gut in Mathematik und Zeichnen sein.
4 In 2040 ________________ thirty years old.	2040 **werde ich** dreißig Jahre alt **sein**.
5 You ____________________ believe me, but I really like going to school.	Du **wirst** mir **nicht** glauben, aber ich gehe wirklich gern zur Schule.
6 Kim wants to be a hotel ________________.	Kim möchte Hotel**managerin** werden.
7 Swimming in a lake in winter is ____________________.	Im Winter in einem See zu schwimmen ist **verrückt**.
8 It's difficult to make __________________ about the future of our youth centre.	Es ist schwierig, **Vorhersagen** über die Zukunft unseres Jugendzentrums zu machen.
9 Liz ________________ quite a lot of money.	Liz **verdient** ziemlich viel Geld.
10 Juan can ________________ being a nurse.	Juan kann **sich vorstellen**, Krankenpfleger zu werden.
11 Jacob is a __________________ scientist.	Jacob ist ein **erfolgreicher** Wissenschaftler.
12 Dad's predictions never ________________.	Papas Vorhersagen **werden** nie **wahr**.

3 New words and phrases

▸ SB, pp. 150–152 | VOCABULARY pp. 268–269

1	John and his nephew had an interesting __________ about music.	John und sein Neffe hatten ein interessantes **Gespräch** über Musik.
2	Can you give me an __________ for this mess?	Kannst du mir eine **Erklärung** für diese Unordnung geben?
3	What __________ do you do at home?	Welche **Pflichten** erledigst du zu Hause?
4	__________ your T-shirts before you put them in the wardrobe.	**Falte** deine T-Shirts, bevor du sie in den Schrank legst.
5	We __________ our car once a month.	Wir **waschen** unser Auto einmal im Monat.
6	Who __________ in your family?	Wer **wäscht die Wäsche** in deiner Familie?
7	Sometimes Jim has to __________ his little brother.	Manchmal muss Jim seinen kleinen Bruder **babysitten**.
8	Phil earns some money with __________.	Phil verdient etwas Geld mit **Babysitten**.
9	Please __________ the __________ when it's finished.	Bitte **leere** die **Geschirrspülmaschine**, wenn sie fertig ist.
10	Please take the __________ bottles to the bottle bank.	Bitte bring die **leeren** Flaschen zum Glascontainer.
11	Please __________ the living room.	Kannst du bitte im Wohnzimmer **Staub saugen**?
12	We need a new __________.	Wir brauchen einen neuen **Staubsauger**.
13	Your bedroom is a mess! You really __________ tidy it.	Dein Schlafzimmer ist ein Chaos! Du **musst** es wirklich aufräumen.
14	Present your results in a __________ __________.	Stelle deine Ergebnisse in einem **Säulendiagramm** dar.
15	Draw a __________ line.	Zeichne eine **waagerechte** Linie.
16	A bar chart has two __________: an x-__________ and a y-__________.	Ein Säulendiagramm hat zwei **Achsen**: eine x-**Achse** und eine y-**Achse**.
17	Walls are usually __________.	Wände sind normalerweise **senkrecht**.
18	Molly grew up in a __________ family.	Molly ist in einer **großen** Familie aufgewachsen.
19	__________ cooking after work.	**Es macht mir nichts aus,** nach der Arbeit zu kochen.

▸ Check

10

4 Listen carefully!

Höre dir die Sätze aufmerksam an und schreibe das fehlende Wort in die Lücke.

1 It's not easy to make good ______________.
2 Laura, what are your plans for the ______________?
3 I think I want to be a ______________.
4 I won't ______________ as much as a programmer, but that's OK.
5 I don't ______________ working at night.
6 I can also ______________ being a baker.
7 My sister is a ______________ banker.
8 When she was little, she wanted to be a dancer, but her dream didn't ______________.
9 What ______________ do you have to do?
10 I have to empty the ______________.

5 New words and phrases

► SB, p. 153 | VOCABULARY p. 269

1 I tried a ______________ English breakfast when I was in London.	Ich habe ein **typisches** englisches Frühstück probiert, als ich in London war.
2 Forgetting Mum's birthday is so ______________ you.	Mamas Geburtstag zu vergessen ist so **typisch für** dich.
3 Asif's family has a ______________.	Asifs Familie hat einen **Eckladen**.
4 We wanted to go to the park. ______________ it started to rain.	Wir wollten in den Park gehen. **Genau dann** begann es zu regnen.
5 I want to ______________ my old bike and buy a better one.	Ich möchte mein altes Fahrrad **verkaufen** und mir ein besseres kaufen.
6 We ______________ our car because we don't need one.	Wir **haben** unser Auto **verkauft**, weil wir keines brauchen.
7 So far we ______________ 100 tickets for the school concert.	Bisher **haben** wir 100 Karten für das Schulkonzert **verkauft**.
8 On school days I get up very ______________.	An Schultagen stehe ich sehr **früh** auf.
9 Let's ask a ______________ to bring you the dress in your ______________.	Lass uns eine/n **Verkäufer/in** bitten, dir das Kleid in deiner **Größe** zu bringen.

6 New words and phrases

▸ SB, p. 154 | VOCABULARY pp. 269–270

1	The Christmas concert was a ____________.	Das Weihnachtskonzert war ein **Hochgenuss**.
2	Let me ____________ you to a nice piece of cake.	Lass mich dich auf ein schönes Stück Kuchen **einladen**.
3	We need to ____________ for food today.	Wir müssen heute Lebensmittel **einkaufen**.
4	We spend about twelve ____________ of our money on food.	Wir geben ungefähr zwölf **Prozent** unseres Geldes für Lebensmittel aus.
5	A few ____________ will make the hall nicer.	Ein paar **Spotlights** machen den Flur schöner.
6	The high energy costs are ____________ ____________ again.	Die hohen Energiekosten **stehen** wieder **im Blickpunkt des Interesses**.
7	Do you want to ____________?	Möchten Sie **bar bezahlen**?
8	Where is the nearest ____________ ____________?	Wo ist der nächste **Geldautomat**?
9	I ____________ in the morning.	Ich **gehe** morgens **mit dem Hund raus**.
10	You ____________ hit other children.	Du **darfst** andere Kinder **nicht** schlagen.
11	I have £250 in my ____________.	Ich habe 250£ auf meinem **Sparkonto**.
12	Grandma collects ____________.	Großmutter sammelt **Münzen**.
13	I have some money in my ____________.	Ich habe etwas Geld in meinem **Sparschwein**.

7 What are the words: *That's when – That's why – That's what – That's how?*

Setze die richtigen Wörter in die Sätze ein.

1 Sam is very helpful. ________________ everybody likes him.

2 You finished your homework before you watched TV? ________________ it should be.

3 A good friend – ________________ everybody needs.

4 His dog fell into the river. ________________ Tom screamed.

8 What are the words: *must, mustn't* or *don't have to?*

Setze die richtigen Wörter in die Sätze ein.

1 You ________________ walk the dog. I've already been in the park with him.

2 You ________________ buy a ticket before you get on the bus.

3 You ________________ eat sweets after you have brushed your teeth.

4 You ________________ be successful as long as you're happy.

5 You ________________ leave the door open when you leave the house.

▸ Check

9 New words and phrases

▸ SB, p. 155 | VOCABULARY pp. 270–271

1	Molly wants to ________________ her desk yellow.	Molly möchte ihren Schreibtisch gelb **lackieren**.
2	Be careful with the ________________.	Sei vorsichtig mit der **Farbe**.
3	Our ________________ sells delicious cakes.	Unsere **Bäckerei** verkauft leckere Kuchen.
4	________________ need to get up very early.	**Bäcker/innen** müssen sehr früh aufstehen.
5	Rishi works in an ________________ shop.	Rishi arbeitet in einem **Elektronik**geschäft.
6	The ring was a ________________ from my aunt.	Der Ring war ein **Geschenk** meiner Tante.
7	Before we go home, I want to buy a few things at the ________________.	Bevor wir nach Hause fahren, möchte ich ein paar Dinge im **Souvenirladen** kaufen.
8	Jane is a ________________.	Jane ist **Zeitungshändlerin**.
9	Lara buys sports magazines at the ________________ near her house.	Lara kauft Sportmagazine im **Zeitschriftenladen** in der Nähe ihres Hauses.
10	Our new sofa is very ________________.	Unser neues Sofa ist sehr **bequem**.

10 Word search

Finde acht Verben im Wortgitter und kreise sie ein. Vervollständige dann die Sätze mit ihnen. Achte dabei auf die richtige Form des Verbs. Verwende jedes Verb nur einmal.
Suche in diesen Richtungen: ↑ → ← ↗

V	W	A	S	H	E
B	U	I	L	D	K
F	O	L	D	M	A
N	E	A	R	N	B
S	E	M	P	T	Y
M	U	U	C	A	V

1 Tarek ________________ his bedroom once a week.
2 Bankers ________________ quite a lot of money.
3 Grandpa ________________ our house forty years ago.
4 Tyler has to ________________ the dishwasher.
5 Do you like ________________ cakes?
6 I'm a bit tired. I ________________ just ________________ lots of clothes.
7 We ________________ our house last month.
8 ________________ your hands, please. They're very dirty.

11 New words and phrases

► SB, p. 156 | VOCABULARY pp. 271–272

1	__________ the dress?	**Was kostet** das Kleid?
2	__________ the shoes?	**Was kosten** die Schuhe?
3	Are you looking for a special __________?	Suchen Sie nach einer besonderen **Marke**?
4	__________ help me, please?	**Könntest du / Könnten Sie** mir bitte helfen?
5	Can I __________ this dress, please?	Kann ich bitte dieses Kleid **anprobieren**?
6	There's a __________ over there.	Dort drüben gibt es einen **Umkleideraum**.
7	Here's your __________.	Hier ist Ihr **Wechselgeld**.
8	Do you need a __________?	Benötigen Sie eine **Quittung**?

12 Lost words

Vervollständige die Sätze mit den Wörtern aus den Luftballons.

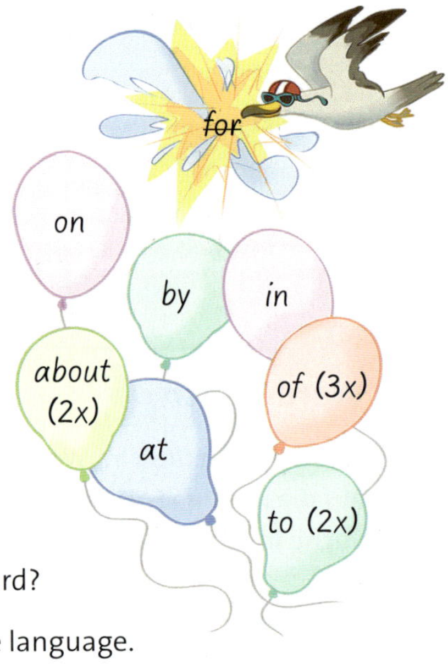

1 We have to shop *for* clothes next week.
2 I'd like to try these trousers __________.
3 It's hard to make predictions __________ the weather next month.
4 My brother is crazy __________ football.
5 Sue is __________ the hairdresser's.
6 Molly is typical __________ her age group.
7 Can you please explain this exercise __________ me?
8 Do you want to pay __________ cash or __________ card?
9 Thirty per cent __________ my friends speak more than one language.
10 Mum treated me __________ a big piece __________ cake in a nice cafe.

13 Different sounds

Welcher Vokallaut klingt anders als die anderen in der Reihe? Unterstreiche das Wort. Suche dann zu jeder Reihe zwei passende Wörter im Kasten.

1 nurse – clear – earn – word __________
2 rule – school – know – move __________
3 chore – course – hour – bored __________
4 treat – sleep – beach – bread __________
5 gift – big – five – hill __________

bean • door • false • fifth • hurt • learn • moon • new • three • trip

► Check

14 New words and phrases

► SB, p. 157 | VOCABULARY p. 272

1	We can't buy the house. The ______________ is too high.	Wir können das Haus nicht kaufen. Der **Preis** ist zu hoch.
2	Grandma always sends us a ______________ when she's on holiday.	Oma schickt uns immer eine **Postkarte**, wenn sie im Urlaub ist.
3	Is it warm enough to wear ______________?	Ist es warm genug für **die kurze Hose**?
4	Sam is our best ______________.	Sam ist unser bester **Kunde**.

15 New words and phrases

► SB, pp. 158–159 | VOCABULARY pp. 272–273

1	"Where is Tom?" – "He ______________ shopping."	„Wo ist Tom?" – „Er **ist** einkaufen **gegangen**."
2	"Where is my bag?" – "I'm sorry, it ______________."	„Wo ist meine Tasche?" – „Tut mir leid, die **ist weg**."
3	My grandparents live far away. I really ______________ them.	Meine Großeltern leben weit entfernt. Ich **vermisse** sie.
4	The bus was late, so I ______________ the first lesson.	Der Bus war verspätet, sodass ich die erste Stunde **verpasst habe**.
5	We'll ______________ Brighton soon.	Wir werden bald **nach** Brighton **ziehen**.
6	It's ______________ beautiful day. Let's go to the beach.	Es ist **so ein** schöner Tag. Lasst uns zum Strand gehen.
7	"Do you know the way to the library?" – "______________ me. I'll show you."	„Kennst du den Weg zur Bücherei?" – „**Folge** mir. Ich zeige ihn dir."
8	You only do this to ______________ me.	Du machst das nur, um mich zu **ärgern**.
9	Sarah has found a good job in London. She wants to be ______________ her parents.	Sarah hat eine gute Stelle in London gefunden. Sie möchte **unabhängig von** ihren Eltern sein.
10	Ken has made a ______________ of fruit salad for the party.	Ken hat eine **Schüssel** Obstsalat für die Party gemacht.
11	Ken's parents have their own ______________.	Kens Eltern haben ihren eigenen **Betrieb**.

16 New words and phrases

▶ SB, p. 160 | VOCABULARY p. 273

1 Sorry, I can't hear you. The ________________ is bad.	Tut mir Leid, ich kann Sie nicht hören. Die **Verbindung** ist schlecht.
2 I can ________________ my phone ________________ my printer.	Ich kann mein Mobiltelefon **mit** meinem Drucker **verbinden**.
3 Can you ________________ your phone number, please?	Kannst du bitte deine Telefonnummer **wiederholen**?
4 Olivia's ________________ is her creativity.	Olivias **Stärke** ist ihre Kreativität.
5 Tarek is very ________________ because he does a lot of sport.	Tarek ist sehr **stark**, weil er sehr viel Sport macht. 
6 I can't ________________ the puzzle.	Ich kann das Rätsel nicht **lösen**.
7 Usually there is more than one ________________ to a problem.	Meistens gibt es mehr als eine **Lösung** für ein Problem.

17 Listen carefully!

11

Höre dir die Sätze aufmerksam an und schreibe das fehlende Wort in die Lücke.

1 We ________________ our car last month.

2 My new walking boots are very ________________.

3 There's quite a lot of money in my ________________ ________________.

4 I want to be ________________ of my parents.

5 Let's get some fresh bread from the ________________.

6 There's a ________________ outside the supermarket.

7 About twenty ________________ of adults in Britain cannot read or write well.

8 Alfie and Tess want to start a ________________.

9 Please ________________ your family name.

10 One of Alfie's ________________ is that he is a good listener.

▶ Check

18 New words and phrases

▸ SB, pp. 162–163 | VOCABULARY pp. 273–274

1	Sarah always ______________________ the weekend.	Sarah **freut sich** immer **auf** das Wochenende.
2	I ______________________ ______________ from you.	Ich **freue mich darauf**, von dir **zu hören**.
3	I didn't have any flour to bake a cake, but ______________ our neighbour had some.	Ich hatte kein Mehl, um einen Kuchen zu backen, aber **glücklicherweise** hatte unser Nachbar ein bisschen.
4	Do you believe in ______________?	Glaubst du an **Horoskope**?
5	Do you know your ______________?	Kennst du dein **Sternzeichen**?
6	Sarah's ______________________ is very good.	Sarahs **Aussprache** ist sehr gut.
7	How do you ______________ your family name?	Wie **spricht** man deinen Nachnamen **aus**?
8	If you don't know a word in another language, you can look it up in a ______________.	Wenn du ein Wort einer anderen Sprache nicht kennst, kannst du es in einem **Wörterbuch** nachschlagen.
9	Mia is an ______________ child.	Mia ist ein **fantasievolles** Kind.
10	Our neighbour is ______________________ everything that goes on in our house.	Unsere Nachbarin ist **neugierig auf** alles, was bei uns im Haus vor sich geht.
11	Luckily my parents are very ______________ ______________ my taste in music.	Glücklicherweise sind meine Eltern sehr **tolerant gegenüber** meinem Musikgeschmack.
12	Moving to another country means a ______________ change for children.	In ein anderes Land zu ziehen bedeutet eine **dramatische** Veränderung für Kinder.
13	Do you have any ______________ experience in babysitting?	Hast du **praktische** Erfahrung mit Babysitting?
14	My parents are ______________ people. They often invite friends.	Meine Eltern sind **kontaktfreudige** Menschen. Sie laden oft Freunde ein.
15	Sarah's friends are very ______________.	Sarahs Freunde sind sehr **großzügig**.

19 Picture crossword

Sieh dir die Bilder an und trage die richtigen Wörter in das Gitter ein.

1

2

3

4
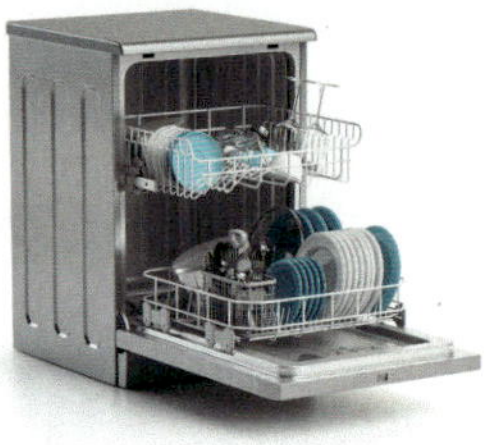

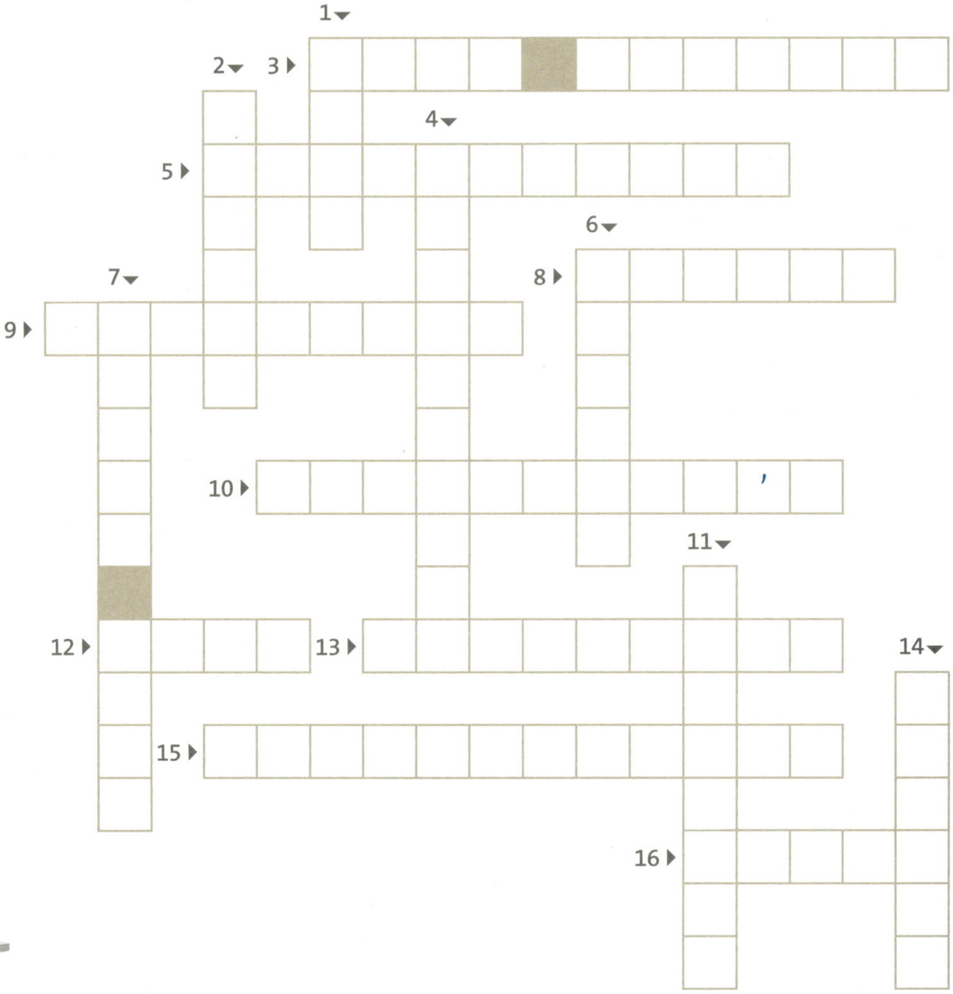

5

6

7

8

9

10

11

12

13

14

15

16

▸ Check

20 What are the words?

Schreibe auf, was gemeint ist. Manchmal musst du mehr als ein Wort schreiben.

1 (to) shop for sth.: ______
2 a talk between people: ______
3 (to) take the dog for a walk: ______
4 a present: ______
5 (to) say something again: ______
6 a shop that sells cake and bread: ______
7 the place in a shop where you can try sth. on: ______
8 (to) make somebody a bit angry: ______
9 a machine that cleans your dishes: ______
10 a place where you can buy magazines etc.: ______

21 What did they do yesterday evening?

► SB, pp. 312–313 (irregular verbs)

Vervollständige die Sätze mit dem *simple past* des Verbs in Klammern.

1 **Alfie:** My parents ______ (go) to a concert, so I ______ (babysit) my little brother.

2 **Tess:** I ______ (spend) the evening with two friends. We ______ (make) cupcakes, and I ______ (eat) too many of them. I ______ (feel) a bit sick when my parents ______ (come) home.

3 **Ella:** I ______ (have) band practice yesterday evening. I ______ (sing) some new songs.

4 **Rishi:** I ______ (be) at home with my grandpa. He's blind, so first I ______ (read) the newspaper to him, and then he ______ (tell) me some very funny stories from the past.

22 Opposites

Finde die Gegenteile.

1 dependent ◄► ______
2 comfortable ◄► ______
3 tolerant ◄► ______
4 (to) buy ◄► ______
5 (to) pay in cash ◄► ______
6 late ◄► ______

23 Let's talk: Über Berufe und die Zukunft sprechen

▶ SB, p. 226

Ein Freund / eine Freundin, mit dem/der du dich auf Englisch unterhältst, fragt dich nach deinem Berufswunsch, den Berufen deiner Eltern und nach deinen Wünschen für die Zukunft. Erzähle ihm/ihr, was du werden wolltest, als du jünger warst, was du jetzt werden möchtest, welche Berufe deine Eltern haben und wie du dir dein Leben in der Zukunft vorstellst.

Start like this:

When I was little, I ...
Now I ...

My mum is a ...
My dad is a ...

In the future I'll ...
Maybe I'll ...

24 Let's talk: Einkaufen und über Preise sprechen

▶ SB, p. 227

Sieh dir die beiden Bilder an und schreibe zwei passende Dialoge dazu. In Bild 1 bittet das Mädchen (B) die Verkäuferin (A) um Hilfe. Sie möchte die Hose in Größe M und das Kleid in Blau. Sie möchte beides anprobieren. In Bild 2 möchte das Mädchen (B) die Kleidung mit Karte bezahlen und bittet die Kassiererin (C) um eine Tragetasche. Sie bekommt die Tasche und auch eine Quittung.

1

2

A: Can ______________________________?

B: Yes, please. Do you ______________________________

______________________________?

A: I'll go and see if we have them in size M.

What about the dress?

B: Do you have ______________________________?

Shop assistant comes back with trousers and dress.

A: Here you are.

B: Thank you. Can I ______________________________?

A: Yes, of course, the ______________________________

______________________________ are over there.

C: How would you like to pay?

B: I'd like ______________________________.

C: OK. Put your card here, please.

B: I'd ______________________________, please.

C: No problem.

B: Can I have a ______________________________, please?

C: Sure.

B: ______________________________.

C: Bye.

▶ Check

°Unit 6
The treasure hunt

1 New words and phrases

▸ SB, pp. 176–177 | VOCABULARY pp. 274–275

1	Did you enjoy the ____________?	Hat dir die **Schatzsuche** gefallen?
2	____________ are very important.	**Naturschutzgebiete** sind sehr wichtig.
3	Jack has a ____________ garden.	Jack hat einen **hübschen** Garten.
4	____________ if you need help.	**Ruf**, wenn du Hilfe brauchst.
5	There are lots of ____________ in our park.	Es gibt viele **Wege** in unserem Park.
6	Mr Cox ____________ the class ____________ five groups.	Herr Cox **teilte** die Klasse **in** fünf Gruppen **auf**.
7	Jamie ____________ under his bed.	Jamie **versteckte sich** unter seinem Bett.
8	These ____________ will help you to solve the puzzle.	Diese **Hinweise** helfen dir, das Rätsel zu lösen.
9	There are lots of flowers ____________.	Es stehen viele Blumen **entlang des Weges**.
10	At the beginning of the school year, Ms Hill ____________ the books ____________.	Am Anfang des Schuljahres **händigte uns** Frau Hill die Bücher **aus**.
11	________________________.	**Viel Glück!**
12	Do you know any ____________?	Kennst du irgendwelche **Abzählreime**?
13	I couldn't find my pen, so Liz gave me ____________.	Ich konnte meinen Stift nicht finden. Deshalb gab Liz gab mir **ihren**.
14	The football fans ____________ "Go, Dave, Go!"	Die Fußballfans **sangen** „Los, Dave, los!"
15	Please don't feed the ____________.	Bitte füttern Sie nicht die **Enten**.
16	Molly ____________ move to London.	Molly **beschloss**, nach London zu ziehen.
17	Don't cycle ____________ a helmet.	Fahr nicht **ohne** Helm Rad.

2 Scrambled words

Hier sind einige Buchstaben durcheinandergeraten. Schreibe die Wörter richtig auf.

1 Last year Sam went to the Lizard *utrNae veseRer* in Cornwall. ____________

2 He also visited the *eyprtt* village of Mousehole. ____________

3 The village is no longer a *dhiden etrreasu*, but full of *urisotts*. ____________

3 New words and phrases

► SB, p. 178 | VOCABULARY pp. 275–276

1	"What's your name?" asked the girl and ________________ me.	„Wie heißt du?" fragte das Mädchen und **zeigte auf** mich.
2	When it's hot, we jump into the ________________ behind our house.	Wenn es heiß ist, springen wir in den **Teich** hinter unserem Haus.
3	In the morning Molly ________________ her horse to the field.	Morgens **führt** Molly ihr Pferd zur Weide.
4	Tom ____________ the visitors to the museum.	Tom **führte** die Besucher zum Museum.
5	Let's hide behind the ________________.	Lass uns uns hinter dem **Busch** verstecken.
6	I didn't hear the ________________.	Ich habe die **Klingel** nicht gehört.
7	Please don't walk on the ________________.	Bitte den **Rasen** nicht betreten.
8	____________________. There is a parrot.	**Schau nach oben**. Da ist ein Papagei.

4 New words and phrases

► SB, pp. 179–180 | VOCABULARY p. 276

1	Rabbits feed on ________________.	Kaninchen fressen **Löwenzahn**.
2	Let's sit down on the ________________ over there.	Lass uns uns auf die **Bank** dort drüben setzen.
3	Sam tried to ________________ the ball.	Sam versuchte, den Ball zu **fangen**.
4	Yesterday Jack ________________ a lot of fish.	Jack **hat** gestern viele Fische **gefangen**.
5	Liz works in a car ________________.	Liz arbeitet in einer Auto**fabrik**.

5 New words and phrases

► SB, p. 181 | VOCABULARY p. 276

1	______________________ your wedding.	**Herzlichen Glückwunsch zu** eurer Hochzeit.
2	Cara worked very hard this year and got good ________________.	Cara hat in diesem Jahr sehr hart gearbeitet und gute **Ergebnisse** erzielt.
3	At the end of the concert the audience ______________________________.	Das Publikum **klatschte** am Ende des Konzerts.
4	______________________________!	**Wir haben es geschafft!**
5	Sam and Tom are ________________.	Sam und Tom sind **Mannschaftskameraden**.
6	You mustn't ________________ in a test.	Du darfst bei einem Test nicht **schummeln**.

► Check

6 Listen carefully!

12

Höre dir die Sätze aufmerksam an und schreibe das fehlende Wort in die Lücke.

1 Tim's parents have prepared a ______________________ for his birthday party.

2 They ______________________ some things in the park behind their house.

3 They wrote some clue cards and ______________________ them ______________________.

4 When all the guests were there, they ______________________ them ______________________ three groups.

5 Tim's father ________________ one group, his mother ________________ another group.

6 Tim's group didn't need a ______________________. Tim often plays in the park ______________________ his parents.

7 First they went to a ____________ where they found a box of chocolates under a ____________.

8 Then they walked through the ________________ and jumped over some ________________.

9 One of Tim's ____________________ found a clue card under a ____________________.

10 The other children ___________________ their hands and shouted "_________________"!

7 Lost words

Vervollständige die Sätze mit den Wörtern aus den Luftballons.

1 Look ___*up*___ in the sky. Can you see the bird?

2 Let's divide the cake ____________ eight pieces.

3 Max hid ____________ the wardrobe.

4 There are big old trees ____________ the trail.

5 Ms Green handed ____________ the tickets for the show.

6 ____________ the end of the show everyone clapped.

7 Being late is so typical ____________ you, Max!

8 "That's my boyfriend," Cara said and pointed ____________ Sam.

9 I felt ill and decided ____________ stay in bed.

Bye!

Have fun in the holidays

and see you soon

for Wordmaster 3!

ADVANCED lighthouse 2

Wordmaster

Im Auftrag des Verlages erarbeitet von
Ursula Fleischhauer, Hannover

In Zusammenarbeit mit der Englischredaktion
Klaus Unger (Projektleitung), Lisa Ahmadi sowie
Elizabeth Pancake-Steeg

Medienmanagement
Silke Kirchhoff

Illustrationen
Evelt Yanait, Advocate Art
Scout-Illustrationen: Irina Zinner, Hamburg

Fotos
Anja Poehlmann, Brighton
Für die freundliche Unterstützung danken wir der
Varndean School, Brighton

Umschlaggestaltung
Rosendahl, Berlin

Layoutkonzept
Klein & Halm, Berlin

Layout und technische Umsetzung
PER MEDIEN & MARKETING GmbH, Braunschweig

Audio-Dateien
Studio
Clarity Studio, Berlin
Regie und Aufnahmeleitung
Susanne Kreutzer
Tontechnik
Dimitris Kritikos

Druck
Athesiadruck GmbH

PEFC
PEFC/18-31-166
PEFC-zertifiziert
Dieses Produkt stammt aus nachhaltig bewirtschafteten Wäldern und kontrollierten Quellen
www.pefc.de

www.cornelsen.de

1. Auflage, 1. Druck 2024
978-3-06-034604-2

Quellenverzeichnis

Titelbild
Cornelsen/Personen am Strand: Anja Poehlmann, Strandhäuschen: Shutterstock.com/JoolsW

Illustrationen
Cornelsen/Buch-Illustration: **Adrian Barclay**, Torte: Shutterstock/New Africa: S. 1/m.l.; Cornelsen/**Evelt Yanait**, Advocate Art: S. 1/m.r., S. 1/o., S. 1/u., S. 5, S. 7, S. 12, S. 15, S. 20, S. 26, S. 32, S. 52, S. 54, S. 57, S. 58, S. 60, S. 64, S. 70, S. 76, S. 79; Cornelsen/**Irina Zinner**: S. 2/u., S. 23/u., S. 28/u., S. 33, S. 59, S. 79; Cornelsen/Maren Collet: S. 31

Abbildungen
S. 2/m.: Shutterstock.com/New Africa; **S. 3:** Shutterstock.com/Madeleine Forsberg; **S. 4:** Shutterstock.com/Goxy Belgrade; **S. 8:** Shutterstock.com/Stephen Rees; **S. 10/m.:** Shutterstock.com/prapass; **S. 10/u.:** Shutterstock.com/Zhuravlev Andrey; **S. 11:** Shutterstock.com/Pixel-Shot; **S. 13:** stock.adobe.com/goir; **S. 14:** stock.adobe.com/Becky Stares; **S. 16/2:** stock.adobe.com/blazic27; **S. 16/3:** stock.adobe.com/Goffkein; **S. 16/4:** stock.adobe.com/Wayhome Studio; **S. 16/6:** Shutterstock.com/New Africa; **S. 18:** stock.adobe.com/FP Creative Stock; **S. 19:** Shutterstock.com/ABO PHOTOGRAPHY; **S. 23/o.:** Shutterstock.com/Eric Isselee; **S. 25/o.:** Shutterstock.com/Prachaya Roekdeethaweesab; **S. 25/u.:** stock.adobe.com/Alexandra_K; **S. 27:** stock.adobe.com/T. Michel; **S. 28/o.:** Shutterstock.com/Arcady; **S. 29:** Shutterstock.com/Utekhina Anna; **S. 50:** Shutterstock.com/rururu1111; **S. 51:** stock.adobe.com/Melinda Nagy; **S. 53:** Shutterstock.com/BY213; **S. 55:** stock.adobe.com/by-studio; **S. 56/1:** stock.adobe.com/BillionPhotos.com; **S. 56/10:** Shutterstock.com/Moving Moment; **S. 56/11:** Shutterstock.com/Marti Bug Catcher; **S. 56/12:** Shutterstock.com/Waeel quttene; **S. 56/2:** Shutterstock.com/mexrix; **S. 56/4:** Shutterstock.com/FabrikaSimf; **S. 56/5:** Shutterstock.com/AlenKadr; **S. 56/6:** Shutterstock.com/Pineapple studio; **S. 56/7:** Shutterstock.com/Moving Moment; **S. 56/8:** Shutterstock.com/New Africa; **S. 56/9:** Shutterstock.com/Sayouna; **S. 62:** Shutterstock.com/Chepko Danil Vitalevich; **S. 67:** Shutterstock.com/SeventyFour; **S. 69:** stock.adobe.com/Nasared; **S. 71:** stock.adobe.com/simon gurney; **S. 72/m.:** Shutterstock.com/baranq; **S. 72/u.:** stock.adobe.com/Pineapple studio; **S. 73:** Shutterstock.com/Net Vector; **S. 74/1:** stock.adobe.com/Сергей Луговский; **S. 74/10:** stock.adobe.com/Hatia; **S. 74/11:** Shutterstock.com/KANGWANS; **S. 74/12:** Shutterstock.com/Viktor1; **S. 74/13:** stock.adobe.com/DragonImages; **S. 74/14:** Shutterstock.com/SeventyFour; **S. 74/15:** Shutterstock.com/sergey causelove; **S. 74/16:** Shutterstock.com/CarlosDavid; **S. 74/2:** Shutterstock.com/everytime; **S. 74/3:** Shutterstock.com/Hadrian; **S. 74/4:** Shutterstock.com/Maxx-Studio; **S. 74/5:** stock.adobe.com/Rawpixel.com; **S. 74/6:** Shutterstock.com/Africa Studio; **S. 74/7:** stock.adobe.com/AkuAku; **S. 74/8:** Shutterstock.com/Inara Prusakova; **S. 74/9:** Shutterstock.com/Alex Pin